RED VENDETTA

STEWART CLYDE

HUNT PRESS

JOIN THE HUNTING PARTY

Get a FREE, Stirling Hunt Mission, top-secret psychological profile and short story.

Based on true events.

Just tell me where to send it: details in the back of the book.

For Ema

CHAPTER ONE

Hunt sat behind the steering wheel and looked at the General in the rearview mirror. The traffic was blocked and slow moving. He tapped the steering wheel with his thumb. He was impatient and bit the inside of his cheek and bounced his knee. Hunt looked down at the cars again. The red tail light ahead shone in his face. He felt the General's eyes on the back of his neck and shifted uneasily.

Just as the tail lights ahead went dark, a woman wearing a fur coat and hat, collar pulled up against the wind, stepped off the sidewalk and right in front of the car. Hunt stepped on the brake and pressed the horn. More instinct than any real danger of bumping her. She looked directly at him and blew him a kiss, before she mouthed something in a language Hunt couldn't lip read. Her bright red lipstick stuck in his mind. That look she gave him was charged, like clouds before a lightning storm. She was attractive with foreign features, not the pretty roundness of an English girl. Higher cheekbones, with a sharpness to the edges. He watched her cruise across the front of the bonnet. She was confident and dismissive. She walked like she was on the runway. Snowflakes swirled around her, and the wind caught the ends of her Monroe-

1

blonde hair. She glanced away from him and crossed the street and dissolved into the throng of tourists and people in Leicester Square.

Hunt gripped the leather steering wheel more tightly. He regretted his reaction. He'd pressed the horn, not because he was an impatient driver - he knew that about himself already - but because he didn't manage to contain his frustration and he knew the General could see it. This wasn't the assignment Soames promised him, but he tried to remain professional and do his duty to his country and do what was required.

He tried to shake off the feeling of being dismissed or disregarded. Soames had been promoted after the Equatorial Varrissa mission and Hunt now felt like an afterthought. He had been promised help, to try and find out the truth about what happened to his mother. So far he hadn't had any or heard anything.

Hunt felt the impatient eyes watching him again from the back seat. Hunt knew the General felt like he was wasting it in standstill traffic outside the Leicester Square tube station and was eager to get home to his family, but only after something else he felt eager for right now. Like an itch he couldn't scratch. Hunt felt like he was wasting it too, when he could be having a drink alone in a Soho dive bar. The sidewalks were bustling with people, they pushed and jostled and stepped out into the street.

He thought about the blonde. She looked Baltic or Scandinavian. She could have been a mistress, or a model. Snowflakes drifted through the neon lights. They hit the windscreen and melted. The steering wheel was cold and he blew into his hands and rubbed them together. The intermittent *whoomf* of the wiper blades removed the melted snowflakes from existence.

"How long have we been together now?" the General asked from the back seat. He was formal and stern and took himself seriously. Hunt checked his watch and then wondered why he'd done that. It wasn't as if he had been counting the minutes they'd been together. Despite his misgivings about the mission he'd come to admire, and quite like, the General. He realised the General had his flaws, but what man doesn't? The General had been kind to him during his time as his personal close security, which meant more like personal assistant and chauffeur, than bodyguard. He'd also gotten to know the General's family and Hunt had been invited to the birthday party of the youngest child. Hunt was the giant the kids tackled in the yard.

"Just over six months, General."

"Any family in London, Hunt?"

Hunt knew there was a depth to the question. Like an iceberg floating below the surface. Hunt never spoke about his family. His father, or his mother. He dared not think about them most of the time, let alone try and explain it to his superiors, no matter how closely they lived and worked together. Maybe he had a fear of getting close to people, or people getting close to him.

"No, sir, not really," he said, and almost to himself, "No family anywhere."

"It occurred to me the other day that you know almost everything about me, and I know almost nothing about you ..."

Hunt's head shook once involuntarily as he thought about it. The General could have asked him more questions, but then again, Hunt could have been more forthcoming. Hunt always thought the General was disinterested, or cagey. Maybe it was Hunt who was cagey.

"Nothing much to tell, General. I just go where I am told and look after who I am told. It's the way I like it," he lied, and forced a smile into the rearview mirror.

Silence.

"How good are you at carving turkey?" the General asked.

3

Properly to himself this time, "I'm better at carving up a man."

"Sorry, what?"

"Just saying my grandfather used to carve the turkey in our house, with an old plug-in electric carving knife."

"This Britain's man in Rhodesia you're talking about?"

"Sir?" Hunt looked back in the rearview mirror at his passenger. Did the General mean his grandfather was a British spy?

The General looked out the window. "Never mind. Listen, Stirling, we'd love to have to you over for Christmas at ours. If you don't have any other plans, of course."

"Oh, no sir, thank you, but you haven't seen the family alone in so long."

"Think it over. It's a standing invitation. Really. The boys love you and if you cook the meat like the last time ... Karen would have you over any time."

There was a sudden thud on the door. Hunt turned quickly and reached into his jacket for his Sig Sauer P220 pistol and touched the grip. A drunk Father Christmas had stumbled into the side of the car. He raised his hand and pulled a drunk face in apology. Hunt watched him as he meandered off. There was a knock on the glass. Hunt spun around again.

"It's okay," the General said and pressed the button on the door. He dropped a purple twenty pound note into the Father Christmas' gloved hand. The beggar's eyes lit up and the smell of cider from his breath hit Hunt's nostrils.

"God bless you! God bless you ..." the man said and his voice faded as the window wound itself up.

"You know where we're going, don't you, Hunt?" and then as Hunt pulled forward, said, "Oh, there we are, traffic's moving ..."

Hunt inched the car forward and stopped again.

"You know where it is, don't you?"

4

"Yes, sir," Hunt said.

"It's just across the square, over there," the General pointed with his leather-gloved hand, "I'll jump out here and meet you. Keep this for me won't you?"

Hunt turned. The General leaned forward holding out a small navy blue box. "It's just a gift for the wife, Hunt. Nothing to worry about. I'll get it from you a bit later, but I don't want to forget it in that place, or for the girls to think I bought it for them, if you see what I mean?"

Hunt took the box from General Patrick. The General opened the car door and Hunt heard the rush of wind and traffic noise.

"Thanks old boy... " General Patrick said. "At least it means you don't have to go shopping for me to buy the whole family presents this year, doesn't it!" and laughed as he leaned to get out of the sedan. General Patrick stepped out of the car before Hunt could say anything biting in reply.

The General pushed the door shut. There was a comforting thump and it was silent once more. General Patrick pulled the collar of his coat up and skipped through the traffic. He lifted a hand and apologised to a tuk-tuk rider he'd cut off as he crossed the street and disappeared into the knotted Christmas crowd.

Hunt sighed and shook his head and leaned forward on the steering wheel. Traffic moved again and he inched forward. He looked at the navy box. Intrigued, he opened it with a click. Hunt saw a diamond encrusted Bremont Hawking Quantum ladies watch glistening in the neon light. He was impressed. It seemed like the General had turned a corner. He was paying attention to his family for the first time since Hunt knew him.

General Patrick held power and influence in the defence community. His official title was the United Kingdom Chief of Defence Staff's Liaison Officer to the US Chairman of the Joint Chiefs of Staff. Which meant that his office was next door to the United States Chairman of the Joint Chiefs. The man who advised the President of the United States. The most powerful man in the world. A man with the power to start a nuclear war. General Patrick, by extension, was privy to top secret information shared with the President of the United States. General Patrick reported directly to the Prime Minister of the United Kingdom. Another world leader in charge of a nuclear arsenal.

General Patrick had just returned from Washington DC to be with his family for the holidays. Wife Karen and their two boys, eight year-old Charles, and seven year-old Damian. And, the first thing he wanted to do was visit his favourite girl at his favourite Chinatown brothel. He'd also probably *still* want Hunt to go shopping for presents at Hamleys to alleviate the inevitable guilt he felt once the fantasy receded. Hunt tapped the steering wheel. He was fidgety. His elbow still hurt. Psychologically he'd struggled. His night terrors had been growing worse. Drowning, or waking up paralysed and thinking there was a stranger in the room. He pulled out the sleeve of pills. One of the side effects of amitriptyline, ironically, was nightmares. That, amongst other drugs he was self-medicating with, to control his post-traumatic stress symptoms. He swallowed a tablet and took a deep breath.

HUNT REMEMBERED how he'd looked out over the river Thames, from high up in the Secret Intelligence Service building. It was spring then, and the sun shone through the glass and warmed the skin on his arms. There were riverboats full of tourists on the Thames, and children eating ice-creams on the street below.

"You know General Sandford don't you? Or, Brigadier

Sandford, as he would have been back then," Soames asked him.

Hunt turned from the green windows and went to the long conference table and sat down. Soames was in his traditional grey double-breasted suit. It was a Friday, so he'd 'dressed down' with a baby blue coloured tie covered in cartoon farm animals. He'd noticed Hunt looking and said, "My granddaughter picked it out for me ..."

Hunt dropped the corners of his mouth and nodded, "Looks great. Really suits you."

"Anyway," Soames said, "You were telling me about General Patrick Sandford. Do you know him?"

There was a knock at the door and a caterer wheeled in a tray of coffee and biscuits.

"Thank you," Soames said. She nodded and placed the tray on the conference table and hurried out.

"No," Hunt said, "You were asking me about him. I only know him from reputation. We've never crossed paths."

"Okay. Good."

Hunt picked up a ginger nut and broke it in half and popped it in his mouth. The stale crunch of Government-sponsored cookies reminded him of emergency rations in a war zone.

"Why?" Hunt asked through the taste of ginger biscuit.

Soames poured him a glass of water and pushed it in his direction.

"General Patrick is taking over as the Liaison Officer to the Joint Chief."

Hunt shook his head. "Punchy role," he said and took a sip of water to clear the crumbs.

"Positively slips off the tongue," Soames said.

"What does it mean?" Hunt asked.

"It means that he has moved up the ranks very, very quickly," Soames said. He looked at his tie and brushed lint away.

7

"And, it means he is in a very high profile position as the inside man, if you like, for all of the biggest of bigwigs at the head of the Armed Forces, and represents the United Kingdom in the United States, in front of the Joint Chiefs of Staff."

"Which means?"

"God, really Hunt! Which means, he has a direct line to the President."

Hunt laughed.

"I know that part, what I mean is; what's the *so what*?"

"Ah, good. The so what is, we have reason to believe him to be a target."

"You think he is compromised?"

"No, I didn't say that, I said we believe he may be a target."

"What sort of target?"

"That's the mission. To stop him being compromised, if he's ever approached. He has a *reputation*. Just make sure he doesn't get himself into trouble. Don't let him get caught on camera urinating on a lady of the night or something. If you notice anything out of the ordinary, report it to us. That's it. Easy peasy."

"Go on …" Hunt had another try at the biscuit.

"You'll be assigned to him as close protection."

"Baggage handler, you mean."

"Not if you do your job properly. Your bootneck backstory might help … Endear you to him. He won't know your true role. It'll just be warrior to warrior, and all that."

Hunt chewed his biscuit.

"Keep a close eye on him, gain his trust. It'll give you some time in America, you can develop your network, now that you want to be a real spy …"

Soames grinned, and Hunt dropped the biscuit in disgust and shook his head. He wiped his hands.

"Could be fun, you never know, although the Redskins aren't any good," Soames said.

HUNT DECIDED he'd had enough. The General was taking liberties. Hunt wasn't comfortable being this far away from him. Frustrated by the slow moving traffic, he checked his wing mirror, put it in drive and revved the engine hard and ramped the pavement. The car hopped onto the curb and he found a space on the yellow lines, hoped he wouldn't get a ticket, but it was good enough for now.

He left the indicator warning lights clicking on and off and climbed out and into the crisp nighttime air. He took off briskly. The fast walk turned into a jog. The soles skidded as he slid them on the stone slabs across Leicester Square and moved between clumps of tourists and shoppers. The brothel was called *Shishi-shishi*.

When he got to the edge he turned left and looked down the red-lamp lined lane and into Chinatown. Chinese lanterns hung from the streetlights on either side of the cobbled brick street. It was busy with crowds of Asian people walking back and forth chatting and eating the noodles out of paper pots. He moved quickly again towards the brothel. He felt uncomfortable having left the General alone. It was only the second time in the past six months the General had been out of his sight. Soames had been very clear with him that the Clubhouse thought the General might be a source of an intelligence leak, or vulnerable to being compromised. What Hunt was witnessing tonight set off alarm bells. The General was highlighting just how his personal tastes and deviant activity could make him susceptible to blackmail from some influential state, or non-state actor.

Hunt's job was as a layer of protection to make sure that the General couldn't be influenced by people with a social engineering agenda. What havoc could a state wreak if they had a video of a General Patrick, and more importantly, what intelligence would the General be willing to give up to stop it getting out? It was a senior position and he was being groomed for the top job. The most secret agency in the Secret Intelligence Service weren't taking any risks.

Hunt saw the brothel. It had a yellow and red sign offering Chinese herbal medicine and massage. He pushed the door open and walked into a tiled waiting room. It looked like a cheap hotel reception. White tiled floors, low ceiling with purple neon lights running the length of the room. The smell of lavender gave it a midnight aura.

Hunt saw the General standing in the foyer with a tall Chinese lady. The madame, no doubt about it. She was a slender woman with dark bobbed hair that looked like a wig. She wore a black gown with a diamond choker around her throat.

"Hello Patrick!" The woman said and air kissed his cheeks, "How are you darling?" she asked and fingered the choker. Hunt stepped forward and they both looked. The Chinese madame leaned into General Patrick's left ear and whispered something. She had a devious smile on her face as she withdrew and looked Hunt up and down.

"Do you know this man, Patrick?" she asked as she turned and moved gracefully behind the desk.

"Yes, this is my age-stealing handler," General Patrick said while he continued to look at him. "Hunt, this is Madame Sue, wait here until we've concluded our business." He turned back to Madame Sue and said quietly, "Is she ready for me?"

"Ready and waiting for you, General," she said.

"Good. Hunt, here, keep hold of my coat."

He took it off and tossed it in Hunt's direction. Hunt looked up at the ceiling and took a breath. He was sweaty from the jog and he didn't like the idea of sitting in a brothel waiting room. In the meantime he was probably getting a parking ticket or a clamped wheel.

"Take a seat, Mister Hunt," Madame Sue said and took the General by the arm. "I have a special surprise for you

Patrick. We have your favourite girl, the French one, Antionette waiting for you upstairs, but special surprise for you, I have complimentary availability for another. I think you might like. Two for the price of one, what do you say Patrick?"

"I see you haven't forgotten to take care of your special clients ..." General Patrick said and gave her a sideways glance. His influence was one of the reasons Madame Sue hadn't been raided by the Metropolitan Police over the years. High-up friends in high-up places.

"You are my special customer Patrick, and I have the most special relaxing medicine for you."

They disappeared from view.

Upstairs, General Patrick followed Madame Sue and watched her slender buttocks move as her silk gown shimmered. She led him to the Opal Room, an exclusive suite. The one he always used. She opened the door and he felt the coolness of the conditioned air. The suite was large and very clean and comfortable. There was a four-post bed in the middle and the windows were blacked out with a picture of a purple sunset over a shoreline.

Sir Patrick undid his tie and Madame Sue pressed a small red button on the wall. She summoned the girls.

"You won't believe this new girl, darling," she said. She ran her hand down his back and pulled his tie off and it slipped from under his collar. "Her profile is simply tailor-made for you, Patrick. She is all the way from the old Eastern block, via Athens. She has just arrived in London. Completely fresh and brand new, if you know what I mean."

He did. And, he couldn't wait to relax. The tension and stress he felt from the past six months on the job in Washington had taken its toll. He had no release. No way to get rid of the stress and pressure that followed a high-profile position like a shadow. And such a public posting. He wasn't sure how much longer he could do it for. He would have to talk to his wife. God, his family. He tried to put it out of his mind, but they were always there. Added to it all, he had to try and ignore the other shadow that followed him around and listened to his every word. Some sort of Secret Intelligence Service grunt. He wasn't even sure if Hunt was his real name. He assumed not. General Patrick was ready to relieve the tension and glad to visit Madame Sue's establishment. It was the one pleasure he continued to allow himself, even as a young lieutenant.

Madame Sue slipped out and closed the door. A red light blinked above a concealed door along what looked like a built-in cupboard.

"Come in," Patrick said.

A shutter lifted automatically and revealed two women standing in a brightly lit bathroom. They were both in lingerie, the bottle-blonde one wore black, and Antionette with black hair, wore red. The blonde was taller, more slender, smooth pale skin, bright red lipstick and sporting an open fur coat draped on her shoulders.

"I hope with nothing underneath," General Patrick chided. The girls entered and circled the General and caressed his torso as they moved around him.

"I have heard a lot about you, my dear. What should I call you?"

She leaned in and bit his earlobe and said, "Natalia."

The General couldn't place her accent. Not Russian. Something else. He wanted to ask where she was from, but Antionette pushed her finger to his lips. He grabbed her hand.

"Hello, General," she said. He lifted her hand and kissed it. She had been a favourite of his for the last few years. He never tired of her.

"Pour us a drink will you," he said to Natalia. She moved over to the bar and Antionette told her, "The General likes absinthe."

Natalia poured the green liqueur into three crystal glasses, dropped a block of ice in each, placed a sugar cube on top of the absinthe spoons and poured ice-cold water over the lumps of sugar. It melted and activated the herbaceous aroma of the French alcohol. She walked back to the bed with the opalescent-cream coloured drinks.

"Why don't you take your clothes off ..." Antionette said. She was being suggestive and the General liked it.

"Why don't *you* take my clothes off?" the General retorted and she replied with a naughty laugh and a smile. Antoinette slid off the bed with her elegant legs and went to the cupboard and pulled out a whip and put on a black leather military cap.

"This is what you wanted, wasn't it General?" She said and cracked the whip. General shivered. God, I've missed this, he thought.

"Your drink, General," Natalia said.

He turned to look at her and took the green drink from her hand.

"Shall we make a toast?" Antoinette asked.

"To wives and lovers," General Patrick said, "And never the twain shall meet." He laughed at his member's club joke and the girls smiled and took a sip and tasted the liquorish flavour.

The General knocked his back in one shot. The potion worked its magic and they all relaxed. Natalia still seemed tense, but she was easing into it. The next few minutes were a blur of bodies, lingerie, ties and shirts strewn across the room. Natalia removed his watch. Antoinette handcuffed the General's hands behind his back, and both girls started to rub his body. He moaned with gratification and laid further back. He felt elated. This is what he had been waiting for. Over six months of torment trudging the offices of the Chairman of the Joint Chiefs of Staff in Washington and all the while listening to top-secret reports. He shook his head to clear his mind. He had two, young, supple and beautiful women and they were in charge. They kissed each other in front of him.

Suddenly, Natalia pulled away and said, "I just need to go to the bathroom. I'll be back in a second."

Antoinette nodded and continued to pleasure the General alone.

When Natalia came out of the bathroom she was fully dressed in a black leather catsuit. She picked her fur coat up off the floor. General moaned again and, through the pain, noticed she was dressed.

He halfheartedly mumbled, "Where the hell do you think you're going?" in between gasps. Antoinette looked up from her work on him. She furrowed her brows in confusion. The tall blonde put on her fur coat, fixed her lipstick in a small mirror, and then pulled out something that looked like an epinephrine auto-injector. Both the general and Antoinette looked at her and stopped what they were doing.

"What the hell is going on?" Antoinette said.

Natalia swung a high-heeled boot and connected with the side of Antionette's jaw. She screamed and sprawled backwards off the bed. The General moved to get up, but the chains clanked against the headboard as they pulled tight. He was still handcuffed.

She climbed on top and mounted him. She put her thighs on either side of his waist. General Patrick struggled. She pushed him down and held her hand on his neck and said, "This is a gift from Anatoly ..." General Patrick struggled and said, "No, no, please!"

Natalia ignored him. "You have failed to live up to your promise and now we will take what we want, without you ..." The General wriggled again and tried to flip over. Her dancer's thighs were powerful. She lifted the auto-injector and plunged it into the side of his neck. He writhed and convulsed. Seconds later he was violently sick on the purple bedding. He shivered uncontrollably as his body seized up.

"Goodbye, General," she said sweetly.

His eyes bulged out of their sockets. The veins in his neck and temples popped out. His face was blood red and ballooned. He frothed at the mouth. His eyes pleaded with her. Natalia picked up the General's briefcase, blew him a kiss, and silently closed the door.

CHAPTER TWO

Madame Sue was behind the reception desk. She stood opposite Hunt and flicked through a glossy magazine. She occasionally looked up and caught his eye and gave him a wire-thin smile. Her face then changed to one of strained politeness, no doubt because she had this hulk sitting in her waiting room.

"No pretty girls for you?" she enquired of Hunt and flicked the page.

He shook his head. "No, thank you."

"You do like girls, don't you?" she asked incredulously.

"I do, actually, yeah."

She sniffed. Hunt and Madame Sue both looked up at the same time as the *clattering* of high heeled boots came down the corridor. Madame Sue looked surprised as the tall blonde with red lipstick glided past her. Hunt's eyes followed her to the door. He recognised her. This was the same woman who he'd nearly run over with the General's car less than an hour ago. She turned as she got to the exit and blew him a kiss and then burst out of the bright yellow doors and into the cold snowy London night.

"Who was that girl?" Hunt asked Madame Sue.

"New girl, very naughty. Meant to be with Patrick right now!" she said.

She picked up the telephone and dialled a number. No reply. She hung up. Visibly upset, she bit the corner of her fingernail. Hunt sat and looked on. The briefcase. "Try it again," he said.

There was no answer and Madame Sue shook her head. Hunt jumped up quickly. He dropped the coat. His heart thumped hard. His instinct told him something was very wrong.

"What room and what floor?" Hunt demanded.

Without arguing, Madame Sue handed him a spare key and said, "VIP room, Opal Suite, top floor."

Hunt sprinted. He took the stairs two at a time and burst through the doors into the top-floor corridor. He swivelled his head and looked for the door and saw the gold plaque. The key card didn't work. He tried it again and again. Finally, the green light shone and the mechanical lock unwound. He burst into the room.

The lights were off and he slid his palm along the wall to find the switch. He found it. The lights gradually glowed and lit the room. A slender, pretty, black haired girl sat on the floor at the base of the bed and rubbed her jaw. Hunt saw the General on the bed. He was facing away. Hands cuffed to the bed, and a syringe sticking out of his neck. Hunt smelled a strong sour stench. He ran to him.

"General!" Hunt yelled, "Wake up!"

Hunt pulled the syringe out of his neck. Saw vomit. It smelled like the General had defecated in his trousers. Not unusual after someone has died. Hunt felt for a pulse anyway and slapped him to try and wake him. There was no response. And no pulse. Hunt's mind raced. Fifty thoughts at the same time. Should he call an ambulance? Or chase the blonde out into the snowy streets?

She would be long gone. Hunt pulled out his mobile

phone. He needed to contain this situation, immediately. He dialled the duty phone number and Tom Holland, his new handler, answered.

"Tom, it's Hunt. Listen, I've got a situation. General Patrick is lying on the bed with his trousers around his ankles, a syringe sticking out of his neck, and a sheet covered in blood and vomit and piss and he isn't breathing. He has been poisoned. Injected with something. We are off Gerard Street in Chinatown. I need a clean up team, and a hearse, and I need a crew to come and secure the area. This is highly sensitive, Tom, I can explain it all when you get here."

"You'll have to."

Silence.

"Tom?"

"Christ! Oh, Christ ..." Hunt heard him say. "Alright, Hunt. Just make sure you've got the room secured. I don't want anybody in or out, especially if it is what you say ... I'll get our forensic team out. The Met are going to want to get involved, but you need to contain that. Just make sure that nobody goes into that room, no matter what, and I will get our boys over there to analyse the scene. Nobody in, or out, do you understand?"

"I understand," Hunt said and hung up.

"CHRIST," Gerald Soames said. He sat behind his wide, polished-mahogany desk. He was on edge. Tom Holland stood with his hands behind his back in front of the Director of Intelligence's desk. Gerry had been in the high-backed office chair for a little over six months, and he'd fit into the role like he slipped on one of his tailored Saville Row suits.

"The Chief has been on the phone," Gerry said, "The Foreign Secretary has been updated on the situation. Goddamn it ..." He sighed. He raised his fist to his mouth and bit his knuckles as if he was stopping himself from screaming in frustration.

"A General from within our own core defence staff ... assassinated in the middle of central London! If this gets out we are all in for hell this New Year. "

Soames' confidence had grown as he'd filled the role and he felt finally able to exert his mental agility. He'd bloomed into the spymaster he always knew he could be. It was all about to come crumbling down around him, he could feel it. He was already in the twilight of his career, but in controlling a group of case officers, and via those case officers controlling their operatives, he was moving pieces strategically around the chess board of global espionage. Now it was all in jeopardy.

"Christ! This has got right in behind our defences, Tom. How did we not see this? 'C' isn't happy, what the hell happened? I need answers and I need them now."

Tom shifted uneasily and lifted a hand to his mouth and cleared his throat and prepared to speak.

"We don't know, Sir, we're still trying to find out the facts."

"Well what, pray tell, was Hunt doing for goodness sake?"

"It seems the General skipped out of the car. We knew of his proclivities before, but it seems Hunt wasn't able to keep them under wraps."

"Oh, dammit-to-hell!" Gerry banged his fist on the desk. It was a good show. Holland looked suitably agitated.

Soames in turn looked at Holland apologetically. It was uncharacteristic for him to lose his cool and he knew it. He was sure Holland got the message.

"I must say, Sir ... Hunt did a really good job, given the situation. It seems like the Metropolitan Police and the National Crime Agency are cooperating.

"Well, they've had word from the Foreign Secretary, no doubt," Soames said.

"But, it's delicate. Hunt managed to guard the door to the General's suite with his big frame and threatened anyone who tried to come past him. We managed to get our people to arrive before the police and secure the scene. They made it look like a natural death. They're saying heart attack to the media, but not where it happened. Just that it was near Leicester Square."

"Do *we* know anything ... Anything else at all?" Soames asked. Anticipation and tension seeped out of him.

"No sir," Holland said and swallowed.

"There were no cameras?"

Tom frowned. "The establishment's clientele, you can imagine, aren't fans of having themselves captured and recorded on closed circuit television. We do have a statement from the madame, and from the other girl in the room, unfortunately the details they had ... it's a fake name, no address, no identification."

"How do you know it's fake?" Soames asked.

"Checked the databases, no hits," Holland answered. "Doesn't exist."

"I wouldn't think brothel owners are too careful about keeping records of the girls," Soames said. "That doesn't mean it's not her name, it just means that we have no record of her ..."

"Yes, sir. This one apparently came highly recommended. We're trying to find out details of who she was recommended by. Hunt seems to think that she was Eastern European of some description, tall, blonde, red lipstick. Beautiful by all accounts."

"And deadly."

"What we were thinking, sounds extreme, but fits the *modus operandi*," Holland stroked his chin.

"A sparrow," Soames said and hung his head.

"Or, at least, one of the sparrow school of espionage," Tom said. Soames nodded in agreement. It didn't look good.

"The sparrows have been decommissioned for almost fifteen years," Soames said. "And then, just like that, one turns up in London. How can that be?"

"Also," Holland added, "the General's watch and briefcase is missing ..."

Soames frowned. He thought about this for a moment. His thinking face meant he looked down and put his hand over his mouth and stared into the carpet.

"Do you think General Patrick could have planned to meet her there, for reasons other than sexual appetite?" Soames asked and looked back at Tom. "As in, the General was compromised. Was she a contact from the other side and the meeting went deadly?"

Tom shrugged. "It's a possibility. We aren't ruling anything out right now."

"You sound more like a tit-headed Bobby talking into the camera about a mugging than a Secret Intelligence Officer," Soames said. "Just be straight with me. It's both our lives and careers on the line here, not just yours."

"We need to know what was in that briefcase and we need to know what the hell he was doing there," Holland said. Finally, he was blunt and abrupt enough to satisfy Soames.

"Bloody-well find your operative, Holland. I want to speak to Stirling Hunt right bloody now."

CHAPTER THREE

Hunt walked with his head down and collar up against the wind and sleet. He pushed his hands deep into his jacket pockets. He stopped walking for a moment to look at the Christmas lights that lit the way down Oxford Street. As he admired them, a group of drunken revellers stumbled past him arm-in-arm wearing mini-skirts and high heels and Santa hats. One of the girls blasted a party popper in his face and laughed with a snort. They ducked through a large glass door and disappeared behind the noise into a dim, laser lit night-club. It wasn't the traditional Christmas Eve he remembered fondly from childhood. Hunt kept moving. He was on his way to the only dive bar he knew would be open. He needed to drink - alone - and think.

It was a Spanish-themed pub on a dirty side street. Hunt saw the backlit red sign and the painted red frontage, and pushed himself into the grim, dingy place. Bradley's Spanish Bar was what all central London pubs used to be. Small, cramped, and dark. It smelled of beer and urine cakes. A few of the regulars looked up as he stepped in. He stamped his boots on the mat and shook off the wetness. The bartender wandered over as Hunt removed his black coat.

"Stirling," he said and put out his hand. Hunt shook it. "We haven't seen you in a wee while," Ginger said, and then, "What'll it be, usual?"

"Yes, please."

"Anything in particular?"

"Doesn't matter ..."

Ginger turned to go. He had a Glaswegian accent, by way of East London. He was as tall as Hunt, with a speckled clotted-cream coloured shaved head, and a long goatee beard that hung down 'til it touched the collar of his biker jacket. Hunt wouldn't like to mess with him.

"Wait. Just as long as it's over eighteen years old," Hunt said.

Ginger half-turned and nodded and indicated an empty seat at the bar, "Take a seat anyway and I'll bring it over."

The bartender came up with a tumbler and a small jug of water. He put a napkin in front of Hunt and the tumbler down. He turned again and picked a bottle from the shelf. He poured and held the bottle for Hunt to see. MacCallum eighteen-year-old.

"Let me know if you like it and when you need another," Ginger said.

Hunt lifted the glass in thanks and poured a few drops of the chilled water into the glass and gave it a twirl. Anybody who says not to mix water with malt whisky doesn't know what they are doing. He sniffed it deeply and felt the peat and salt air from the west coast of Scotland in his nostrils. The water released the smells deadened by the bottle after the eighteen years it had spent lying in oak. He took a sip and closed his eyes and felt the burning sensation on his lips, on the tip of his tongue, and concentrated. Smoke. Hearth. Dust. Betrayal. Revenge. Angst. As the flavours dissipated, and his saliva mixed with the liquid, he let it drip down the back of his throat. Like water over a cliff. He gave a little cough and cleared his throat. The bartender watched him and

Hunt nodded his thanks. Ginger went back to polishing glasses.

Alone again. On Christmas. Just lost a man who I was getting close to. Close for Hunt, anyway. He wasn't close to anybody. The mission was, protect General Patrick. Failed. The mission was to protect Queen and country. The country that he loved. Failed. He sighed. He felt heavy. His body ached and old injuries made him want to gripe. Stiff upper lip.

There was a weight on him. The tinnitus in his ear was getting worse. Hunt pumped the fist on the arm where he'd been bitten by the assassin beetle. It still hurt. He'd lost weight since it happened. Not sleeping. Every time he went to a new place his stress and anxiety levels went up. Dreams were busy. Flashes of the desert and hot sun. Taliban fighters jumped out of the closets. Not in a good state. Maybe Gerry was right. Maybe the operation with General Patrick had been a good thing at the time. That was over now. Another choice needed. What was it he was going to do next? Stay or go. There was a charter fishing boat in Mozambique with his name on it.

Hunt felt a blast of cold air as the door to the pub swung open. Hunt took a swig to finish the drink and stood up to leave. He glanced at the entrance and saw a tall man in a Fedora and cream trench coat.

"Damn it," Hunt swore under his breath.

Soames stood in the entrance and shook out his umbrella and removed his scarf. He looked up and saw Hunt and made his way over to the bar. Ginger, attentive as ever, moved towards them.

"I was just leaving," Hunt said.

"No, you'll stay," Soames looked at the bartender. "We'll sit over there. Table service?"

Ginger shook his head.

"I'll have what he's having. Just make it a double."

Hunt's eyes followed Soames to the table. He picked up

the tumbler and sucked on the empty glass and put it firmly back on the bar. He wasn't looking forward to this. Soames pretended to read a menu with his coat still draped over an arm.

"Gerry," Hunt said. "Where's Tom?" Hunt was expecting his case officer to be here, not the Director of Intelligence for The Clubhouse.

"Hunt." Soames didn't look up from the menu. "Merry Christmas. Sit down."

Hunt shook his head, more at the sentiment of a merriment around Christmas than the instruction to be seated.

"Smells a bit like I feel inside in here. Piss and chlorine," Soames said

"I'd rather stand."

"Suit yourself." Soames glanced up at him from the menu. "You usually do ..."

Hunt silently scoffed and felt the rage building in his chest. He decided to remain calm. He breathed deeply, and tried to let it go. It was just an indication of how this conversation was going to go.

"What's the matter, Gerry. No Christmas plans?"

"Look," Soames said and looked up at him. "I appreciate the stoicism, in general and in here, but I have to say it ... You really crapped the old bunk on this one, old man. Sorry to say, but this is an extremely unfortunate incident, Hunt."

He could almost see the steam rising from under Soames' collar. Soames, normally cool and with the stiffest of stiff upper lips, seemed shaken. His voice had lost its metronomic meter. He spoke just that imperceptibly bit faster.

Ginger brought their drinks. No cheers and no toast. Soames picked his drink up and gulped it.

"Thanks, Gerry, I wasn't in the mood for small talk either."

Soames took another gulp.

"What the hell happened, Hunt? What the hell happened

..." Soames shook his head and almost seemed to be talking to himself. "We need answers. The Chief is beside himself with rage. You need to sort this out. The Foreign Office is getting involved ..."

"No, Gerry, I'm sorry. I'm out. I'm not doing this anymore."

"That isn't an option here, Stirling. You don't leave until this is sorted. You don't leave until I say so. So tell me again ... What the hell happened?"

"Don't rile me up like that, Gerry," Hunt answered and they locked eyes. Hunt wasn't going to look away first.

"If I knew what happened, I would tell you. I don't know Gerry, what can I say? We need to find out *why* general Patrick was targeted. We need to find out why they waited ..."

Soames had a curious look on his face. Hunt turned and glanced around the pub.

"Why they waited until we were back in London ..." Hunt said quietly.

Soames shook his head. "This whole incident has put me in quite a mess. As you can imagine, the top floor are very perturbed that this can happen here. We simply need more information. We need more than we have ... and I'm not sure that you're telling me everything there is to know." Soames took another drink.

"What are you saying, Gerry, are there some sort of alternate truths that I'm not aware of here?" Hunt asked.

"Well, maybe, we just don't know..."

"What about footage?" Hunt asked.

Soames shook his head.

"No, I didn't see any functional security cameras in the place either," Hunt said.

"None that we're aware of..." Soames said. "Did Patrick give you anything?"

Hunt was quiet for moment.

"Well, we need all the goddamn footage from the streets

surrounding Leicester Square and the brothel, immediately," Hunt said and looked at Soames with disdain. He could see what Soames was thinking, 'so you do care'.

Soames took another smug sip of his drink.

"What about the surrounding tube stations?" Hunt asked. "Any footage?"

"The whole area around Madame Sue's was blacked out, no cameras, no visuals of any kind. Whoever pulled this off planned it so that they could come and go without being seen..." Soames said.

"Were the cameras hacked?" Hunt asked. He shook his head and squeezed his fist tight. He could feel himself being reeled in. He didn't like it.

"No sign of any attack," Soames said.

"And the girl? Part of an assassin ring ..." Hunt said. "Was she working alone, or part of a team?"

"These are the questions we need answers to," Soames said. "Tom says you got a good look at her?"

A better look at her than he would've liked. She was striking. Devastatingly beautiful. And, a killer.

He nodded. "Yes, I did. When did she start working there? What records are there?"

"There is very little we know right now..." Soames said. "That's why we need you on this, that's why we need your help to try and identify the gaps in the information we have. You are the only one who's seen her. This is going to get very serious, very quickly, and we need you to put a stop to it. I need to debrief you about something. Top secret. About the General."

"Christ, Gerry, can't you people leave me alone?"

"It's the least you could do after getting us into this little situation," Soames said.

And there it was, Hunt's eyes locked with Soames'. He felt the anger rise from his chest into his throat. Soames moved uneasily on his chair, like Hunt might be about to do something violent.

Soames swallowed and pressed on. "Am I wrong? You weren't with him, were you?"

"No, you're right, Gerry. I wasn't there. You should cancel me. Put me on a burn notice."

Soames smirked. "Put it right, Hunt. It's what Kelly would have wanted, isn't it?"

Hunt sat up straight and stared into Soames' face. His eyes darted across the bloated cheeks and stretched skin, which pulled ever tighter over the expanding chin. He looked for some sort of expression. Some emotion. Some sign that Soames knew the importance of what he had just said. Something to tell him that Soames had just said what he thought he had heard. Hunt hadn't heard her name mentioned in over a decade. Why had he brought her up now?

"How do you know about her?" Hunt said. He was blunt and to the point as ever.

"Never mind that. I mean, what did you think? You think we don't know? We know everything about you ..." Soames said. "You need to come and be debriefed properly. We need to run a psychological profile. Polygraph. Drug test. And then, I can share some of what General Patrick was into."

Hunt spun the tumbler on the table in front of him. "Don't talk about her anymore," he said more calmly than he thought it would come out. He hadn't told anybody about his fiancée, Kelly Armstrong. He hadn't told anybody about how she'd died in a terrorist bombing of the American Embassy in Tanzania all those years ago. Had he told anybody? No.

He wondered how Soames knew ...

Did it even matter? Now, he truly had no secrets.

"How was he killed?" Hunt asked. "The General."

"Early analysis says Proton-2020. Radiation poisoning."

"The Russians," Hunt said. "It has to be. Who else has the capability? They've done it before, in London."

"Has to be ..." Soames agreed. "And, by the way, my boy, I would love to leave you alone," Soames said changing tack. "I would love for us to be able to call it a day, because you know, with all the operations we've been on together, Hunt, I understand how it can get so goddamn exhausting. So, yes, I would love to let you drift off into the sunset, but unfortunately you're the only one, at least the only one who has claimed to have seen this blonde assassin ... so unfortunately we need you, and you need us, if you get my drift. We need you on this. Find out why they targeted General Patrick, what we lost in terms of information, and whether they're going to continue killing people for whatever it is they are after. Wouldn't it be the least General Patrick expected? I understand that you're close with the General's wife?"

"What's that supposed to mean ... are you trying to imply something untoward?"

"I'm simply suggesting that she would want to see justice done. Like you wanted to see justice for Kelly..."

It's still on my agenda, Hunt thought.

"Doesn't Karen deserve justice? Who's going to give it to her? She needs somebody, somebody like you, who can bring her closure and find out who did this to her husband, the man who provides for a family. Surely you can see that?"

Of course he could see that. Hunt felt like he was being set up. Nothing fit. Why was Soames here? Why wasn't there an internal investigation into what General Patrick was up to? And, why was Hunt kept in the dark about it?

"Is there something at play here that I'm not aware of?" Hunt asked. "Or, am I somehow under suspicion? Are you saying you're going to throw me to the wolves unless I help you?"

Soames nodded, almost imperceptibly, almost involuntarily.

"I think we understand each other perfectly," he said. "Come to the office in the morning. Get debriefed so I can let you know what Patrick was up to. Until then, stay out of trouble and try - for Pete's sake - to stay sober. I need you in good shape on this."

Soames finished his drink and placed it down.

"You off, just like that?" Hunt asked.

"I was getting so tired of your sarky tone and lack of acknowledgement of your role in this immense cluster," Soames said. "I just have to leave."

Hunt almost laughed. Good old Gerry, he thought. Bastard.

"The only thing I have to acknowledge is that you owe me some information for the thing I did in rescuing Lord Langdon. Which you never gave me ..."

"Oh, yes? And what was it that I promised you? To help you find out what really happened to your mother? You know what really happened, Hunt. And you killed the man who murdered her. You're welcome."

"He claimed she was still alive and the body they found in the dump wasn't her."

"And you believed him?" Soames asked. "When did he tell you this ... Sitting on the top deck of his boat, at a poker table, just before you sliced his neck? Am I missing something here? Wouldn't you *say*, or do *anything* to try and get the upper hand in a situation like that? He was just messing with your head. You think I know more than you about what's going on here, Hunt?"

"You seem to know a lot more about me than you've ever let on."

Soames shrugged.

"I know nobody says what they mean in this game. I might be slow, but I am realising that maybe you know more than what you're letting on," Hunt said.

"If I do, it's only to protect you ..."

"Well, I'm sick of babysitting missions and looking after

the dignitaries. If you know about Kelly, you know why I decided to do this in the first place."

"You think you decided?" Soames grunted. "You did this because this is what you were born to do. You did this because it's what you want to do. You did this because it's the only thing you can do, and the only thing you're good at. And, you know that Her Majesty's Government, and this country, need people like you, to stop people like that," Soames pointed to the front door, to the outside world, to the sleet and storm and rain as it poured down in the blackness outside. "All of this," he gestured around the pub and the people sitting around them, "All this, is why we do what we do."

"Don't give me some bollocks about the greater good ..." Hunt said.

"That's exactly what it's about. That's exactly what it's about," Soames said. He was emphatic. "And, let me tell you this, if you don't do what we need you to do, when we need you to do it, like this moment right here, the greater good is going to suffer. We need you. So, stop feeling sorry for your-self, and get to bloody work."

He picked up his coat. He put it on and pulled on his brown leather driving gloves. He stared at Hunt while he did it.

"Hey," Hunt said as Soames reached forward picked up his glass. "I'm not finished with that."

"You are now," Soames said. "Go home, Stirling. Sober up."

Hunt watched as Soames walked over to the bar and deposited the glasses. He turned back and sat alone and thought about ordering another drink.

CHAPTER FOUR

Hunt kept drinking. He stayed and had at least half a bottle of the peaty, amber-coloured whisky. He walked uneasily up to the bar and opened his wallet and found he had no money left. He waved a lazy hand at Ginger in thanks and made his way to the door. He pulled the door open and stepped into the cold blustery air, and put his coat on too late to stop from getting wet in the rain. He could see his breath in front of his face and rubbed his hands together and stuck them deep in his coat pockets. He walked past a beggar holding a maroon coffee cup and the man asked him for some change. Hunt pulled a face, and said, "Sorry mate, I don't have any change..." and realised he might be slurring a bit.

"God bless you! God bless you..." Hunt heard the homeless man say as he walked away towards a bus stop. Hunt waited under the white fluorescent light for a late night bus. The last bus of the evening. He kept checking his watch wondering where it was, until he realised that it was Christmas and all the bus drivers were already sitting down for the second course of over-cooked turkey, lumpy mash, and too soft Brussels sprouts.

Damn, he hated Brussels sprouts. They reminded him of

being a young officer. On Christmas, the officers served lunch to the junior ranks. Brussels sprouts became the sailor's weapon of choice. The barrage of sprouts was nonstop. He realised the bus wasn't coming, but still had some energy, he wondered what would be open at this time of night.

After his dressing down from Soames. Questioning his commitment, he wondered if it would be a good idea to stop past General Patrick's house and check on the family. He got it into his head that it was a good idea. It's what General Patrick would've wanted after all, he decided.

He was sure they would be sitting around the Christmas tree and opening presents. He could simply go past the house, which wasn't far away by taxi, and have a quick look in the window to make sure that Karen was okay, and that the children were fine. She might even be happy to see him. He'd probably be invited in for a glass of sherry, or even maybe a port.

It was really coming down. As he walked along the pavement he found a broken umbrella lying in the road, he picked it up and dusted it off and mentally patted himself on the back for having such a good idea. He was confident that it was a good idea to go and check on the General's family. It was the least he could do, considering he was supposed to be the one looking after the General on the night that he was killed. He stopped a lonely black taxi. The cabbie pulled over reluctantly and Hunt got in. No chitchat. Just like he liked it. No amount of whisky was going to deaden the feeling of loss and failure Hunt felt. Maybe he would find some redemption in helping the family.

Hunt used his agency credit card to pay the man. He was in the right neighbourhood. He was soaked from head to toe and his boots squelched as he walked. He checked the numbers on the houses. The houses all looked the same to him. He was looking for number 57, or was it a number 75? He could never remember. He'd actually only been to the house once, and it was before he and General Patrick had left for Washington.

Karen had made a lovely potato bake, and Hunt did the barbecuing because he'd been brought up in Rhodesia, where a wood *braai* was a national pastime. It was a type of cultural pride for him to be able to cook red meat on an open flame. General Patrick had tried to cook on gas, but Hunt got his way, because for him, it was a secret man test, and he didn't want to have any less respect for General Patrick because of his choice of barbecuing technique. The kids loved it. The party was a success.

The rain stopped and he discarded the broken umbrella unceremoniously in the gutter. It had lost all usefulness. He passed number 57. It didn't look right, he didn't recognise it. He remembered a big birch tree in the middle of the front garden. The house was an old Victorian, setback from the road, behind a small green wall, and well manicured hedge. Hunt did wonder how General Patrick could afford such a house on a public servant's salary. He assumed it was Karen's money. General Patrick's wife was one of the top solicitors at one of the top corporate law firms in the City. He arrived outside number 75.

He stood in the cold. He stepped from foot to foot to keep warm and gazed up at the property from the street. The lights were on downstairs. Actually, he noticed that all of the lights in the house were on. It seemed odd. He realised that he was starting to sober up after the walk. And, now he was thinking that maybe this wasn't such a great idea after all. Maybe it was stupid, it probably was stupid. After all, if there's doubt, there is no doubt.

He'd let the scotch go to his head. Then he thought he saw something flash across the top window. A black figure. His senses suddenly heightened. He checked his watch again. It was well past midnight. All the lights in the house were on, but surely all the kids were in bed? He didn't know if Karen told them about their father yet. He doubted it.

Not on Christmas. Surely? He wished he hadn't drunk all of those whiskys. He stepped closer to the house. He moved into position so that he could see the living room. He saw a large well shaped Christmas tree with its lights twinkling and there were presents underneath, waiting for the morning to be opened. Then he saw Karen sitting on the floor, with her legs crossed, on a deep red Persian rug. She was hugging the children. She was in tears. She pulled them tight to her chest. She looked terrified, but it must be the pain of the loss she was feeling, Hunt thought. She must have told them. Hunt felt like an idiot. He turned to go. Stupid. Stupid. There had better be a taxi in his future because there's no way he was walking all the way back to the apartment like this.

CHAPTER FIVE

At home, in South West London, Soames sat in the winter sunroom wearing his robe and slippers and flicked through the Times. The doorbell buzzed and Soames' little white Parson Russell Terrier barked.

"Oh, hush, Reverend!" Soames said and pushed himself out of the chair. He pulled his robe tighter and shuffled to the front door. He pulled it open a crack, felt the fresh blast of cold air, and saw a smart looking young woman in a black trouser suit standing on his doorstep. She held a padded envelope in her slender hands, pink from the cold, and shifted uneasily. She shivered and cold morning mist floated on her breath.

"Um, good morning, sir. I mean, Merry Christmas, Mister Soames, sir."

"Good morning, Merry Christmas to you, young lady," Soames said.

"It's Brown, sir, SIS," and she held out her identification. "I have an urgent package for you. It's been vetted and security cleared. I have instructions that you are to view it immediately. The duty officer said that it was highly sensitive information. Your eyes only."

"Right, well, you better come in then..." Soames said and fully opened the door. He stepped back and arced his arm to welcome her into the house.

"No, sir. Thank you, sir. I have instructions to leave the package and return to the River House. But, it is *imperative* that you watch this video now, sir."

She held it out for him.

Soames took it from her. She looked like she was about to salute. Soames was amused at how flustered she was and he felt sorry for how cold she seemed.

"Permission to, um-uh, leave now ...?" She stammered.

Soames nodded and smiled at her and said, "Permission granted. And bring a coat with you next time."

"Yes, sir, was in too much of a hurry," she said and turned on her heels and hurried away with her arms straight by her sides and head down towards the waiting Range Rover.

"Poor girl," Soames said and looked down at Reverend, who was sitting by the door. The dog cocked his head. "Let's see what we have here then."

Soames went through to the living room and pulled out his clunky, black, secure laptop. He found his reading glasses and perched them on the end of his nose, ripped open the envelope, and felt along the edge of the laptop for the slot. He checked both sides of the storage device and pushed it into the port. The computer whirred and he saw one file on the memory stick. He double tapped it and the video player opened. There was no audio, but the image was unmistakable. Stirling Hunt, the covert operative he had recruited, hired, stuck his neck out for, and brought into the fold at the Clubhouse - now one of the United Kingdom's most secret and effective deniable specialist operations units - was on the screen.

"I don't believe it," Soames said. "I don't ..."

Reverend whimpered. Soames watched his operative as he bounded up the stairs at Madame Sue's *Shishi-shishi* brothel.

The camera flicked to a wide angle of the passage. It showed Hunt stop outside one of the suites. The camera flicked again, this time Hunt was in the room with a dark-haired girl and the General. He kicked the prostitute in the face and she crumpled at the foot of the bed. He stabbed the General in the neck.

"No, no, no, no ..." Soames said through clenched teeth, furious. Reverend looked up at him and whined. "It's okay boy," Soames said and rubbed his ear. The dog lay down with his ears perched forward in concern.

"Christ, I can't bloody believe this."

Soames fumbled for his mobile phone. He took off his reading glasses and rubbed his eyes with the base of his palm. He dialled and the line connected.

"Alpha-Whisky-Bravo-Tango, five-three-seven-two-one, Intelligence Director Soames," he said, and passed security on the encrypted line. "I need a citywide sweep. Operative code-name: Boatman, last name Hunt, first name Stirling, wanted for questioning. Approach with extreme caution. Officers are to make an arrest on sight, in connection with the murder of General Sir Patrick Sanders."

Hunt groaned and looked at the ceiling. His tongue was stuck to the roof of his mouth, he was thirsty, felt too hot, and his brain throbbed. He wasn't in a good way. He lay on a bare mattress, the springs poked him in the back. He didn't even have a pillow.

He never spent much time in his flat and had never bothered to decorate. The flat was in a lovely area of London. The Ministry of Defence owned a concrete-facade block of flats at the top of Portobello road in Notting Hill. The building was sympathetically hidden from view by a row of tall trees; otherwise the local residents' association would have complained bitterly about the industrial, post-apocalyptic design of the low-slung block ruining the look and feel of their streets.

His apartment was as comfortable as his mattress. He only had a few items of furniture. One wooden chair, one dining table, one bowl, one plate, one spoon. And one miserable looking alley cat that Hunt let use the flat while he was away.

He'd been walking down Portobello Road one day when he'd heard a desperate meowing coming from inside an abandoned shop. Flea, the cat, was stuck between a window and a metal sheet inside a boarded up shop front. Hunt managed to get the caretaker, they went in the back and rescued him, all starved, angry and afraid. Hunt took pity and took him in, but, like Stirling, this cat couldn't be tamed. Flea only returned occasionally through the window that Hunt left open for him, and even then only for five minutes worth of cuddles and a free breakfast, every now and again.

Hunt knew he wouldn't be staying in the flat long enough to warrant decorating it, and getting belongings that he wouldn't be able to get rid of at a moment's notice. His life was volatile, and required him to move often, he didn't want to be in a position where he couldn't drop everything and walk away in ten seconds flat, if he sensed the heat around the corner.

Something else was poking him in his ribs. He rolled onto his side and reached into his inside jacket pocket and pulled out the box that contained Karen's Christmas present from General Patrick. He put it on the sideboard and then remembered, with a groan, going to the family's house last night. He slapped his forehead with his palm. Stupid. He realised he would have to go back there today, pay his respects, see the children, and give Karen a departing present from her murdered husband. He wondered how much she knew about what happened. Not a great day to be this hungover. Flea scratched and meowed at his bedroom door. Hunt took that as a sign that it was time to get up.

HUNT CLIMBED off the red London bus and rounded the corner onto the General's street in Putney. His head was down, lost in his murky, muddled thoughts. When he looked up he saw the luminous blue and yellow panelling of four Metropolitan Police cars and a police van, parked in front of the General's house. This wasn't good. As he approached the perimeter a young Constable stopped him.

"What's going on?" Hunt asked and raised his chin towards the milieu. Police officers trampled over and mucked up the grass as they moved from the house back to their tented operations centre.

"Move along, please," the Constable said and looked past him.

"I know the family," Hunt said. The Constable's face softened. "We don't know yet. Disturbance of some description last night. Now, move along, please."

Hunt saw the tall Tom Holland, with his arms crossed, as he spoke to a senior looking uniformed police officer.

"I know him," Hunt said absentmindedly to the Constable and lifted his arm and stood on his tiptoes and yelled, "Tom! Tom Holland!"

Holland stopped speaking and turned to look. Holland said something under his breath when he saw Hunt. He apologised to the police officer and walked briskly towards the cordon.

"Tell them to let me in," Hunt said to Holland.

Tom stopped and signalled to the policeman. The Constable lifted the tape and Hunt ducked underneath it.

"Much obliged."

Hunt jogged up to his case officer and Holland turned to walk back to the house.

"Christ, it's cold! You look uneasy," Hunt said to Holland. "Are you alright?" Holland glanced at him.

"Where have you been?" Holland asked, his nose and cheeks were red from the air. "I've been trying to reach you all morning."

Hunt patted down his jacket. He didn't know where his phone was.

"Sorry, I got held up. What's going on Tom?"

"The General's wife and kids were accosted last night. *Someone* broke into their home. Ransacked the place. Children and Karen tied up in the living room. You don't know anything about that, do you?"

Hunt's mind flashed with the image of them hugging and crying on the floor. Hunt put his arm across Holland's chest and stopped him.

"I was here last night, Tom. I saw them through the window." Hunt checked himself. He realised that he sounded panicked. Not a good day to be dehydrated and incomprehensible.

"Are you armed?" Holland asked.

Hunt squinted. What a question, Holland must know he was.

"Are you telling me you did this too?"

Hunt was momentarily stunned by the question, his foggy alcohol soaked brain was slow to take Holland's meaning. And then he realised.

"Oh, wait, no. You think I did this? No. No. What? Of course not!" Hunt gave an uneasy laugh.

Holland's face relaxed and he let out a sigh, "Okay, good. What were you doing here? And when was this? You're all over the wire."

Hunt furrowed his brow, confused, and then heard a shout

from a plainclothes policeman, "That's him, the guy from last night! Same clothes and everything."

A group of policemen and women moved towards Hunt and surrounded him.

"I am sorry, sir, we're going to have to take this man for questioning," the plainclothes officer said to Holland. Holland opened his mouth to protest, but the Inspector turned to Hunt. "If you'll follow me, sir, to the van over there," and indicated the waiting wagon.

Hunt raised his hands to show he wasn't a threat and followed the officers to the van. The inspector pointed to the back seat with the antenna of his hand-held radio and Hunt climbed in.

"Wait here," he said and then shouted over to another plainclothes colleague, "Bill, it's the lad from last night."

Bill was a greying man with a chubby neck and a few days of salt and pepper growth on his face. He ambled over. When he got to the van door he said, "Right. I'm Chief Inspector Talbot and this is Inspector Meeks." He indicated his colleague, and Meeks nodded. "Who are you?"

"Stirling Hunt, I was with the General when he died." The Inspectors glanced at one another.

"We have eyewitnesses that put you here, at the scene, at the same time as the crime took place."

"I was coming to pay my respects," Hunt said. They looked at each other again.

"What, at midnight on Christmas Eve?"

Before he could answer, Holland pushed between the two men. "Excuse me, gentlemen."

"And who the hell are you?" Bill demanded.

Holland reached into his jacket pocket and awkwardly flipped open a black wallet that contained his Secret Intelligence Service identification. Bill took it and studied it.

"I need a word with my man, if you don't mind," Holland said and put out his hand.

Bill handed the wallet back to him and said, "He's one of yours is he?" Holland nodded. "Five minutes," Bill said holding up five fingers, "And then I need to speak to him, *capisce?*"

The inspectors stood within sight, and watched the van suspiciously, as they conversed. Holland turned to Hunt when he was sure the policemen were out of earshot.

"Hunt, I've been told to bring you in. It seems there's some compromising footage from the brothel."

Hunt's face squished up and shook his head. What?

"Gerry, told me last night that there was no closed circuit," Hunt said.

"We thought so too, but it seems like now, there is ..."

"Well, maybe that's good, *if* we can identify the killer," Hunt said. Holland swallowed and shifted uneasily. He put his hand on the roof of the van. Hunt felt trapped.

"Wait, compromising to whom?"

"Just tell me, what were you doing here last night, Hunt?" Holland said. "These coppers want to question you in connection with the burglary of General Patrick's house. You're a suspect. They think you did it. Just tell me you didn't, so I can speak to them, and we can get the hell out of here ..."

"I told you I didn't. Why the hell do they think I had something to do with it?"

Holland's face told Hunt that he was afraid. Stalling. Why?

"They had an unmarked car watching the house as a precaution after the General's assassination. Standard operating procedure, I suppose. A high-ranking family is top of the list for protected assets."

Hunt sat silent for a moment. Holland turned to look at the inspectors, and Bill tapped his watch. Hunt's mind was a blur. He felt short of breath and jumpy. His leg bounced. Holland had a strange look on his face, and his body position cut off any exit. Hunt took a quick look over his shoulder through the back of the van. He saw a woman trying to parallel park in an emerald Mini Cooper.

"So ...?" Holland said as he turned back to Hunt.

Stirling thought about the watch. Should he tell Holland? The gift for Karen. Things were too strange. None of this made sense. Hunt hadn't seen any recording devices in the brothel. So, how was there footage? And, if it backed up what happened ... Why this intensity and the barrage of questions?

"Listen, Stirling, General Patrick was carrying some highly classified and highly valuable intelligence with him back from the United States. Right now, it's missing, and we want it found. We have no idea if it is lost, stolen, or whether we are compromised. So, if you know *anything*, I need you - Christ, Gerry *needs* you - to tell me now. Before we lose control of this situation ..." Holland said and looked nervously around again. "I shouldn't even be telling you that."

"I came, um ..." Hunt was going to tell him. He'd decided. Better to be honest and explain it away, than try to guess what was going on, and what was being said behind his back. *General Patrick gave me a watch to look after for his wife*, he rehearsed how he was going to say it in his head. Now it even sounded odd to Hunt. If it sounded strange to him, how would it sound to these bureaucrats? Just then, Holland glanced over his left shoulder at a line of policemen in high visibility yellow jackets walking towards the van. Holland pulled a face, and Hunt instantly knew they were coming for him. This was a set up, and he was trapped.

"Sorry, Tom," Hunt said as he jumped off the seat and hit Holland in the Adam's apple with the edge of his palm. Holland went down clutching his throat and made a grating garbled sound as he tried to suck in air.

"Hey! Get him!" Hunt heard as he leaped from the police van. Another Constable guarding the other side of the taped perimeter turned, but he was too late. Hunt dropped his shoulder and knocked the policeman over. Hunt stumbled over the body and tore through the police tape like a running back. There was a brouhaha behind him. Hunt was frantic and he could see long streams of his hot breath as he stumbled and ran.

"Stop, or we'll shoot!"

Hunt kept running head down and bobbed and weaved, just like he was taught in basic, down the tree lined pavement in southwest London. He spotted the woman still trying to reverse-parallel park her Mini Cooper S. Hunt sprinted up to the car and stopped himself by slamming his body onto the bonnet.

"Out of the car," he said out of breath. His chest heaved. He was afraid.

She screeched, the engine revved, and the rear hit a parked Mercedes-Benz. Hunt pulled open the driver side door and unclipped her seatbelt. She was shrieking as Hunt grabbed her blazer and said, very fast, as if he was ordering a coffee, "Excuse me ma'am. I'm really sorry. I need your car. I'm sure the insurance will take care of it ..."

He pulled her out and she had a look of disbelief on her face as she stood in her tan-coloured tights and high heels. Hunt pulled the door shut as the officers rushed up. He revved hard, put the steering on full lock and wheel-spun the compact car around her and out of there. He saw the policemen on their radios in his rearview mirror, breathing hard and comforting the shaken woman. He raced away, swerving in and out of residential traffic as the sirens blared behind him.

CHAPTER SIX

He pounded on the steering wheel with his palms and roared in frustration. What the hell are you doing!

He knew it was a trap, but part of him wanted to go back ... laugh it all off, and try and rescue the situation. The other part of him knew that it was dire. He was the fall guy in some conspiracy to assassinate a British General and steal whatever was in his briefcase and have it pinned on him. Now, he knew he couldn't trust anyone.

And now, his own organisation, one of the most secretive and clandestine parts of British government, was after him. What was he going to do?

First things first, he had to dump the car. He knew this part of London. No doubt they would have air assets in place within minutes, if they didn't already, satellite too, and he had to avoid capture on closed circuit television, like the average Londoner was up to thirty times a day. The most surveilled city in the world.

He raced down Putney Bridge Road and accelerated hard down the side streets. The engine whined and tires squealed. He kept off the main roads and looked for somewhere to dump the vehicle. At least that young woman would get her car back. It might make for a happy Christmas after all.

The streets were deserted. The sun hadn't really come up. It started to rain. Just what he needed. He pulled into a leisure centre car park in Southfields and switched the engine off. What are you doing? He breathed, he controlled himself. He became aware of his thoughts. He leaned forward and checked for cameras, and climbed out. There was nothing in the boot or backseat of any use. He was cold, he was getting wet, and the rest of this escape was going to be on foot.

He had to stay off the roads. That meant back gardens, jumping over fences, using side streets and alleyways and avoiding being seen. Hunt was a master at this. During the Escape and Evasion Phase of the Special Boat Service selection they ended the exercise without capturing him. The only person to do it in their history. An entire rifle company was the hunter force, employed with dogs, to capture the soldiers on the selection for the Regiment. They hadn't been able to catch him. Hunt was so successful that they had to send a search party out to find him. They employed local farmers to keep an eye out. He'd survived for seven days by stashing himself away on a peaty forest floor and only stealing out of cover to eat scraps from a dog bowl on a farmhouse at night. After a week the owners took the animal to the vet because they were worried. They wondered why their dog was losing so much weight. Eventually, they drove around with a loudspeaker calling his name along with a message confirming that the exercise was over. He'd beaten them. He never wanted to do that again though, if he could help it. In this situation he might not have a choice.

The streets were empty, he was the only one insane enough to be outside in the miserable black cold. Just him and the police officers chasing him. He checked left and right and sprinted across the road and dropped behind a small wall at the side of a tall Victorian house. The lights were on and he could see the family in the living room. There was a side entrance, a large black wooden gate. Hunt reached over the top and unlatched it, then, very gently, eased the gate shut.

He was off the street in a covered bricked pathway running the length of the side of the house and it led to the back garden. He stopped and crouched for a moment to think. What safe place would be open on Christmas Day?

He needed to be concealed for a few more hours, until it was night, even though the sun barely came up this deep into winter. It was more about human rhythms than visibility. He wanted people tired, hibernative and unaware. Just please don't let it snow. I could use a mosque right about now. Or, better yet, what about a synagogue? At least he wouldn't stick out there. Well, at least not as much.

There was only one synagogue in this area of South West London that he knew of. He'd have to cross Wimbledon Park, and he would be doubling back on himself, but that might just work. He doubted the coppers would think he'd head back, more or less, in the same direction he'd just come from.

Only one way to find out. He made his way to the back of the garden, quickly checked his surroundings and made sure nobody was at his back, and hopped the fence into the neighbour's garden. He landed with a thump on his elbow in a pile of wet compost.

SOAMES SAT ALONE at his desk in the dark, wearing his best knitted Christmas jumper. Green with a reindeer on it. He chewed on the cuticle of his thumb.

"Gerry!?" he heard Tom Holland call out. Just the Christmas I wanted and expected, Soames thought. Holland pushed his way into Soames' dark office without knocking. Holland pulled up just inside the room.

"Are you all right, sir? You're sitting in the dark," Holland said.

"It's that kind of crystal clear deductive thinking that's going to help us catch that bastard, Holland," Soames said and swivelled his chair so he sat straight on with the desk. He reached forward and clicked the desk lamp on.

"He got away, sir," Holland said, more to fill the silence than anything.

"For now," Soames replied, "For now." Soames looked at Holland.

"You've seen the video?"

"Not yet," Holland replied.

"Watch it, tell me what you think."

"Will do, sir."

"Sir?" Holland said after a pause. Soames grunted. "Do you really think he did it?"

Soames shook his head. Not because he thought Hunt didn't, or couldn't, but because he didn't know what to make of the situation.

"I have a feeling we're being played, one way or another," Soames said. He stood and went to the window and looked out over Tower Bridge. He interlocked his fingers behind his back. Holland removed his scarf.

"How's the throat?" Soames asked. "Your voice sounds a little warbled and hoarse."

Holland touched his neck involuntarily. "He, uh, hit me pretty hard," he said.

"Yes," Soames said, "he did, but you're lucky he didn't kill you with that strike, from what I've seen of the man. Maybe he's losing his edge ..."

Holland laughed nervously and then stifled it and coughed.

"Sit down, Tom," Soames said. "I need to tell you something."

Holland did what he was told.

"He didn't tell you anything, did he? Before he knocked you down?" Soames asked.

Holland shook his head, "No," he said. "Nothing."

"Well, this is something even Hunt didn't know about his mission. I am about to brief the Chief, so you may as well know but, I can only tell you what you need to know," Soames said.

"Of course," Holland replied and licked his lips.

"The working theory is that General Patrick was doing a trade with an enemy agent and it went bad," Soames said. He was frank and matter of fact and he blurted it out quickly like if he didn't say it fast and all in one go he might not say it at all. Holland stared at Soames like he was trying to work out what language he'd just spoken to him.

"If I may, sir, whose theory is this, and how did you come by this information?" Holland asked.

Soames glared at him.

"Sorry," Holland said and tried to clarify. "What I mean, sir, is, if it was a secret, and the general was so careful, why do we know about it?"

Soames tapped the side of his nose. Need to know.

"The important thing is, we believe General Patrick was a mole. A traitor," Soames said. He left the sentence hanging in mid-air.

Holland looked like he'd swallowed a bug. He coughed and then looked at the floor like he was searching for something he'd dropped.

"That was my reaction too," Soames said. "I couldn't believe it either, but it's true." Soames was conscious to not come across like he was pleading with him to be believed.

"Where is he now? The informant who told us about Patrick being a mole," Holland asked.

Soames ignored the question, but he was impressed that that was the first place his mind went.

"I never said it was a 'he'," Soames said and waited. Holland looked at him and Soames continued, "We believe that General Patrick was killed, assassinated, possibly in collusion with Hunt. We believe he was killed by the contact who was after whatever piece of intelligence Patrick stole from Washington."

"The blonde," Holland said.

Soames stared blankly at Holland; and Holland, bemused, looked back at Soames.

"And, now we're worried the lid is about to snap shut on our hand while it's in the cookie jar?" Holland asked.

"The Americans can't and must never know. We would never recover. Never. In their minds, they are the only ones allowed to spy on other governments and other citizens. They won't tolerate one of our top brass, a liaison to the Chief of the General's Staff no less, being suspected of being a spy."

Holland was silent. "Why're you telling me this then?"

"I thought you should know."

"Are you worried I'm a leak?"

Soames looked confused.

"We've suspected a leak for some time now," Holland said. "If the Americans found out about this after you've told me, you'd know I was the leak. Is that what is going on here?" Holland seemed distraught.

"No, not at all! Calm down, Tom. I'm just trying to say that there are several possibilities in this case and bring you up to speed. One, General Patrick is compromised and whoever assassinated him now has the intelligence. If they don't have it, that's what they were looking for. I am certain of it. A piece of information that was worth killing a British general over. That's only if they didn't get it from the house last night. Other than that, the only possibility is that Hunt has it."

"He could be our mole," Holland said.

Soames nodded.

"What happens if it is Hunt and the intelligence falls into the wrong hands?" Holland asked.

"Make no mistake, Tom, it could be catastrophic." Soames bowed his head and shook it at the thought, "That cannot be allowed to happen."

Holland nodded. He was understanding the gravity now.

"We need to find Hunt," Soames said. "And, once we do, eliminate him."

"Kill him? But, what if he doesn't have it, or isn't the mole?" Holland asked.

"It's too much of a risk. We have to find and eliminate even the possibility. I want you to mobilise all the operatives. The Metropolitan Police are never going to catch him. Not this boy. Not after what we have taught him to do. We need to mobilise air assets, space assets, and we need specialist people hunters. Operatives who will be able to carry out an Executive Action, despite the ability of the target. Understand?"

Holland laughed out loud, "Where the hell are we going to find people able to do that?" The thought sobered him and he stared blankly out of the floor-to-ceiling glass windows.

"Christ! You know I didn't want to have to do this, Tom. You know I would never make this decision if it wasn't absolutely necessary. But, there's too much doubt. The video tape, the story, turning up at goddamn General Patrick's house last night! He's gone off the reservation, I can't protect him anymore ..." Soames said and took a breath and composed himself. "I want a full team in the basement operational by tonight, I don't care how you do it, you will get them out of bed and get them here, and you'll get that operations room up and running. I want Hunt's head on a silver platter by sunrise."

Holland was pensive, and stared out of the window at the lights on the river.

Soames spread his arms, the reindeer on his Christmas jumper stretched.

"Part of the job," he said. It was as close to an apology as Holland was going to get. "We can't trust this guy, Tom. You can't trust a guy who acts like he has nothing to lose."

"Hunt actually has nothing to lose," Holland said. "He's not acting."

HUNT HEARD sirens and saw the flashing blue lights in the darkness. Patrol cars crisscrossed the streets around him. He heard the whirr of helicopter blades as they passed above him. His eyes were attuned to the dark. His breathing rasped. His clothes were soaked, he was cold, but the adrenaline pumping around his brain kept him alert. He climbed over the high black fence which surrounded Wimbledon Park and lay under some wet shrubbery and waited for the moment to move. It came, and he went.

Up and sprinting, he skirted the edge of the fence, kept low and moved fast. How did you get yourself into this mess? You know it's not too late to turn back. I'm sure they would be happy to see you, and at least you'd get a hot meal in a warm blanket. He'd spent more than one night in jail before, and right now, he felt it was a toss-up as to what the worse option was.

He clambered over the steel fence and exited the park on the east side. The roads were dark and deserted and sleet fell in front of the street lights. He kept close to the cars parked on the verge and stopped occasionally between them to take in his surroundings. The gradient grew steeper as he climbed towards Putney Heath. Just then he heard a siren and blue lights flashed past in a blur as the police car headed south at speed. He felt grotty, like a common criminal on the run, nothing more. He stuck to the wall and made his way around the back of the Wimbledon Lawn Tennis Club.

He couldn't wait to be inside, out of the rain, with even the hint of a chance of getting dry. Finally, boots squelching, he approached the synagogue at the top of Queensmere Road. On the other side of the street was Putney Heath; the forest and fields would be good cover if the temple didn't work out. The Wimbledon Synagogue was a square, brick building, with windows running around the outside of the second floor. It had a flat roof, and barely any markings. Almost as if they didn't want people to know that this was a Jewish place of worship. It looked just like the other low-slung blocks of flats that surrounded it. Fine with Hunt. The lights were off and no cars in the parking lot. He went around back to see if there was a fire exit or service entrance. If all else failed he could hide in the big bins.

He was trained to pick any lock on the planet, but without the right tools those skills were useless. He put his hands up to his eyes and peered into the glass to try and make out any security systems in place. He didn't see an alarm. After all, who'd want to break into the synagogue?

He checked under the mat just to make sure no one had left an emergency key. No luck. He wrapped his coat around his fist and punched a hole in the glass. His knuckles crunched against the solid pane and he felt a surge of pain into his forearm. The shards fell to the floor ground and he spun round instinctively to see if anyone was alerted. If any lights turned on in the surrounding flats. Nothing. He was well covered by the lawn of tall trees that surrounded the building.

He reached through and unlocked the door and took one step inside and half expected an alarm to start blasting. He held his breath, but nothing happened. Safe. He let out a sigh. He needed to make a plan. He needed to decide what to do. And then he needed to get out of here.

Hunt was in a large catering kitchen that supplied the temple. He looked around to make sure he was alone and that no-one else was around. He didn't venture out of the kitchen. He checked if there was any food and he found some pastries in the fridge. He was soaked through. He took his clothes off and turned on the big steel six-burner gas oven. He laid his clothes out on the metal trays and slid them into the oven to dry. While they did, he went to the Chef's office and ate a cold pastry. There was a small element heater in the office and he set it to full and shut the door.

He sat and looked at the watch General Patrick had given him. Could this really be it? He studied it closely. The watch looked in one solid piece. He didn't see how he could open it without breaking it. And he would probably need special tools. There was an inscription on the back, it read: My darling wife, on our anniversary. Odd, Hunt thought, for a Christmas present. Hunt whistled quietly to himself.

The diamond encrusted watch made him think of something else. Hunt knew he would need money. More than he had. He couldn't access any of his accounts. They would know where he was within minutes of any withdrawal. He had nothing to pawn, except the watch and it was too valuable. It was his only bargaining chip. He had no stash of hidden art or jewellery. He only had one thing. The number to a safety deposit box where VD had stashed the red diamond for safe keeping. Money for a rainy day. They'd discussed it as their retirement fund. When it was long forgotten and they were too old to be meaningfully prosecuted. Hell, they could buy their own vineyard to retire to as vine pruning ex-soldiers. The number for the off-book safety deposit box was imprinted in his mind. VD would understand, he hoped. Hunt would make it up to him, one way or another.

If you get out of this, boy, you could be gone. Forever. If you get out of this jam-up they'll never find you. He tore another bite of pastry and ran his thumb around the outside diamond encrusted watch face and it reflected orange in the glow of the glowing elements of the heater.

"You're my ticket to freedom," he said quietly.

CHAPTER SEVEN

Hunt sat in the warm orange glow of the heater. He almost felt back to normal. His clammy skin was drier. Not frozen to the touch. He heard a noise. He stopped chewing, immediately sat still and quiet, and listened like a dog listened for its owner. A car. Sounded old.

It pulled up with a squeal of brakes just outside the back door. Hunt stood. He left the pastry hanging out of his mouth and touched his hand to his shoulder holster, and pulled the office door ajar.

He heard a car door creak and slam shut and the indicators blinked orange as the driver locked it. Hunt saw a man in a black hat with a long beard climb the stairs. The old man was holding a brown paper bag in one arm and jangled a set of keys, as he looked for the right one to unlock the door. Then he noticed the broken glass and stopped. He waited. Then came forward and pushed the synagogue's back door open. The man stopped in the doorway.

He must've seen the oven and the red glow from the heater in the office. He looked like a rabbi. Hunt pulled the office door all the way open and the rabbi startled. He saw

Hunt's naked silhouette. Hunt and the rabbi stood in the darkness and looked at one another.

His hand still on the pistol grip, Hunt took the pastry out of his mouth and said, "Come in, rabbi. Oh, and please shut the door behind you, I've just got this place toasty warm."

The rabbi came in slowly. Turned to close the back door and looked up at Hunt again. Hunt just stood there in his socks, underwear and shoulder holster. He swallowed the last of his danish.

HOLLAND'S TEAM of analysts and support staff meandered into the hastily assembled operations room in the basement of the Clubhouse building in London Bridge.

"Come on people! We don't have all night ... let's hustle! If you've been drinking, which I know many of you have, there's the coffee. Make sure you fill up the pot as you use it. It's going to be a long night ..."

Holland clapped his hands as he rallied the troops. The chatting died down. Soames stood in the back of the room with his arms folded and observed.

"Come on people! We have a tier-one priority asset to catch people. I need a three-dimensional map of London on my screen, now! I need eyes in the air, infrared, a satellite link, and I needed them yesterday."

Fingers tapped the keyboards and the din died down. One of the analysts ran for a coffee and a doughnut from the table and went on typing.

Soames nodded to Holland.

"Get me a picture of Stirling Hunt up on the screen," Holland said to a female analyst in a grey hoodie sitting in front of him. The image flicked onto the fifty-inch screen behind him. It was from Hunt's military identification card. He was slim and had a crew cut.

"Listen up people, briefing time. This," Holland said and indicated the picture of Hunt over his shoulder, "Is the target. Stirling Hunt. Codename, Boatman. Until recently, this agency's best asset. He is wanted, and suspected, of the assassination of General Sir Patrick Sanders last evening. He has in his possession a highly valuable piece of intelligence. A matter of national importance. And, we believe, he intends to defect and sell it to, if not the highest bidder, then our greatest enemy. It is imperative that we stop him. So, until further notice, Christmas leave is cancelled, and if you want to get back to your leftover turkey and Boxing Day football, you'd better catch this man."

"Rishi," Soames said from the back of the room, and an elegant, tall British-Pakistani man in his early-twenties stood up, "Give us a briefing on Hunt. Everything you have. Anything that might help us assess what he is up to."

Holland moved to the side and Rishi picked up a clicker from the table.

"Right, listen up guys. From what I've seen so far Hunt should be a difficult one to catch, so we need to get one step ahead of him and then stay there. Stirling James Hunt, born to a British father and Estonian mother in Rhodesia, what is now Zimbabwe. Both parents believed to have been assassinated in a farm invasion-style Executive Action when he was a child. Raised by his paternal Grandparents. Harvey James William Campbell Senior, Commander of the Order of the British Empire, for his services to the Commonwealth; was a prominent ambassador and our man inside the rapidly changing Rhodesian colony. Hunt's then girlfriend Kelly Jane Armstrong, was killed in the al-Qaeda orchestrated blast on the United States' Embassy in Tanzania. He joined the global war on terror soon after. An ex-Special Boat Service Troop Commander, decorated for his actions in Afghanistan, the Boatman is a highly skilled black-ops asset. He was recruited, trained, and put on operations by Intelligence

Director Soames and has been one of our most reliable assets to date."

Rishi checked his notes. He opened his mouth to continue, and Soames cut him off, "Thank you, Rishi."

The young analyst pursed his lips and went to sit down.

"Top briefing from a fine young man," Soames said. "Just one small, but vital piece of information to add. Not in the file, but about the Boatman's mother ... Her maiden name is Hunt. Hunt's father Harvey Henry James Campbell took his wife's name, it was one of her key demands of their wedding. Strange for the time, but makes sense in the context. Carmen Hunt, Stirling Hunt's mother, is believed to have been the main target in the farm invasion and assassination. Not to kill, but to capture. Intelligence sources suggest that not only did she survive the attack, her husband's death was a cover to take her back to Moscow. They were afraid she was being turned, and she was - by us - until the attack. Hunt's mother was a known KGB spy who was playing both sides for as long as she was active. Either, she was a spy and she learned how to get what she wanted, or she knew exactly how to get what she wanted, and so they made her a spy. I suggest the latter."

Rishi raised his hand, "Where is she now?" he asked.

Soames shook his head, "Name changed, identity changed, we just don't know. But, this operation gives us incentive to find out. Where is Hunt going? Why is he going there? And, crucially, how do we stop him? If he is headed east, we need to know, and we need to stop him. Work out what he wants and we can work out what he is going to do. I want all Clubhouse assets active and ready to move at a moment's notice. Everyone on standby."

Holland moved to the front again. He gave Soames a nod.

"Right, you've heard the situation, you've heard the background. Do your jobs and give me everything we can find. The national security of this nation depends on it. Get to work!"

There was a blur of chatting and typing, analysts talked over one another and the din went higher. Soames took his leave and walked out. Holland saw him go and followed him out. Under the low, dimly lit fluorescent lights, Holland stopped Soames.

"Make it happen, Tom," Soames said. "Also, find out where that boor of Hunt's is. What's his name again?" Soames searched for the name, "Johan Van Driebek."

"No sign of him in months," Holland said.

"I don't care. Check the manifests out of every airport in Southern Africa. Every single one."

"Yes, sir. But, don't you think we should focus our resources on Hunt?"

"No, ifs or buts. Who else is Hunt going to go to? Who else does he know? We created this limited world for him. This limited area of operations. So we could control him. So, let's use it to our advantage and get a step up on him. Yes?"

"Yes, sir," Holland said.

"And Tom," Soames poked him in the chest, "He's got forty-eight hours, starting now, if we don't find out what he is up to and get him back in play, the other assets are going after him. All of them. And he is a dead man. Got it?"

THE RABBI STEPPED towards the table.

"And good evening to you young man. Or, Merry Christmas, should I say," the rabbi said.

Hunt moved forward in his boxer briefs. The floor was cold under his socks. He went towards the rabbi.

"Here, Rabbi, let me help you with your groceries." Hunt was surprised by the rabbi's size, he was tall with a big frame. He must have led an indulgent life.

"Why, thank you. And, may I inquire as to the name of

the person who is helping me with my groceries? I see you have helped yourself to my pastries."

"Come on. Come here," Hunt said and ushered to the rabbi towards the metal kitchen table. "I'll take those," Hunt said and took the keys from the rabbi, "And your mobile phone ..."

"What? You want my wallet too? What is this, the stick up? *Oy vey!*"

"You can call me No-one," Hunt said. "That's my name, and who I am to you. And, no, this isn't a stick-up Rabbi... In fact, I'm really sorry, but ... I am a weary traveler and was in desperate need of shelter and some warmth. I'm sure you can understand?"

The rabbi nodded, "Yes, I can understand. I might not agree with your methods, but I can understand."

"Doesn't the Lord help those who help themselves?" Hunt said.

The rabbi seemed remarkably calm. He was rather a large man, he was older, but perhaps he had seen some things in his day. Things that made him calm in the face of danger. His long grey beard hid his features and in the dim light, Hunt couldn't read his expression.

"May we turn on the lights?" the rabbi asked.

"That isn't a good idea."

"I would very much like to see the man who is holding me hostage," the rabbi said. "I can see that you are a big man, I can see that your body is well formed. By your voice I can tell that you are not originally from here. And, I am guessing that you are not Jewish, my son?" He asked, knowing the answer to the question. "If you are some kind of criminal, on the run from the law, I assure you I offer you no harm. If it is indeed only a warm bed for the night, I am able to give you that."

"That's very kind, Rabbi. But, please don't be concerned, I won't hurt you ... as long as you help me. Our national security is at stake. I know that sounds grandiose, but it's true. The less you know the better."

The rabbi said nothing.

"Make yourself comfortable," Hunt said. "I'm just waiting for my clothes to dry, and I'll be on my way."

The rabbi shook his head, "I suppose I should've stumped up for that security system after all ..."

"Better than an insurance policy," Hunt said. Hunt sat on one of the stools at the table with the rabbi. Hunt needed an insurance policy, since he had no security. He shivered. It was still cold in his underwear.

"I think I have a blanket," the rabbi said. "Shall I fetch it for you?"

Hunt thought for a moment and the rabbi stood to get it. Hunt pulled the Sig P220 and waved it towards the stool.

"Sit down, please, Rabbi. I don't need it. Just stay still for a moment, so I can think."

"Oh! You have a gun! And you have no plan? So, this is going well then?" he said. He was sarcastic and unafraid. Like he had seen it all before and didn't mind.

"I didn't plan on an old rabbi walking into the kitchen on Christmas Eve."

"You didn't plan on a rabbi walking into a synagogue?" he asked, and Hunt saw him grin for the first time. "I am going to remember that one for later. The *qahal* will love it. My congregation ..." the rabbi chuckled.

Hunt appreciated the joke, he put the pistol back in the holster. "Like I said, I am just waiting for my clothes to dry and then I need to get out of London. What kind of car do you have?"

The rabbi eyed Hunt up in the dim light.

"You're not taking my car. I won't allow it. You will have to kill me before you take that car."

There was a stony silence. The rabbi was realising what he

had said. Hunt was thinking the rabbi didn't know who he was talking to.

"Let's let that one slide," Hunt said.

The rabbi looked down. "It's my Jaguar X-type," he said. "She's old, and she whines, but she is beautiful. Just like my wife," he gave a sad smile.

Hunt went to the window and looked. It was a maroon Jaguar with a sloping bonnet and round headlights. He thought for a moment and watched the rabbi in the darkness.

"All right, Rabbi. I won't steal your car. But, I need to get out of London tonight. So, you are going to drive me somewhere."

The man was clearly attached to the car, so let him keep it, as long as he got him where he needed to go.

CHAPTER EIGHT

Natalia Sukolova stood behind a uniformed footman. He was in regal dress, like something from Buckingham Palace, and he pulled open the floor-to-ceiling double doors. They were intricately carved and painted white and gold.

Natalia wore a fur hat and coat and strode confidently into Anatoly Mints' office. She carried a black attaché case. Anatoly leaned on the arm of the great leather chair at his desk. He held a framed photograph and resisted taking his eyes off it as the tall blonde strode in. He looked up and said loud and enthusiastically, "Natalia!"

He opened his arms wide and stood to greet her. They kissed three times in the Parisian manner. He indicated a seat opposite. She put the attaché case on the desk and sat down. She crossed her legs to show off her knee-high leather boots. Mints was in a good mood now.

Natalia had seen him in bad moods. He was a large man, overweight, with hands like a logger. When his mood soured, his pockmarked cheeks lit hot pink, and it seemed like storm clouds were rolling in. He'd hit her more than once. The back of his thick tree-feller hands felt like police batons. Anatoly Mints was in his sixties, but he looked older. He set the picture frame back on the mantel and sat down heavily so the padded leather huffed.

"Do you know who that is?" Mints asked her.

She did. He mentioned it every other time she visited her office, which admittedly, was not often. The black and white picture was of Mints with some other soldiers in a trench. It was taken during the Soviet's war in Afghanistan. Mints had his arm around one of the soldiers in the photograph. It was a youthful Vladimir Putin. He was a young man then, but his narrow eyes and straight nose were unmistakable.

"We fought together, in those days. Can you imagine?" Mints said. "I was just a peasant, a poor boy from the Urals, but even then, I knew he was going to be a great man. And now, I have all of this," he leaned back in his chair and opened his arms and looked at the painted ceiling.

She rolled her eyes. The building was, from the outside, an exact replica of Joseph Stalin's Green Grove Dacha. His summer home near Sochi on the eastern banks of the Black Sea. In reality Mints' replica was a compound, complete with airstrip, and a sparrow school. High, reinforced concrete walls, in the Soviet cinder block-style, protected the structure. The main compound looked like a fortress of protruding green concrete rectangles. It was said that the building, and bunker, could survive a direct hit.

It had been carved out of the dense mountainous forests of the Sochi Nature Reserve to the north of the town. And, if the outside was an exact replica of Stalin's summer house, inside it was the palace of Versailles.

Whereas, Stalin had been a simple man, with simple tastes, that reflected the Russian state of the time. Anatoly Mints' had created a fortified compound in his own image, full of grand high ceilings, gold, antique mirrors and all the decadence of the pre-revolutionary French aristocracy. The story was that he'd saved a young Vladimir Putin's life during the Russian invasion of Afghanistan, and, ever since, he'd followed in the slipstream of the unstoppable rise of the Russian dictator.

That was what Natalia heard, and the legend that Mints cultivated. Only Anatoly and Vladimir knew the truth. One thing Mints had done better than anyone was remain close to the dictator, while maintaining the six degrees of separation he needed to fly under the radar.

That photograph was the only thing to link Mints to Putin and he relished the idea that he was low on the list of sanctions worthy oligarchs and members of the inner circles of state apparatus, even though it was doubtful that anyone wielded as much indirect power in the whole of Russia as he did.

The relationship worked for Putin too, it was deniable, and he trusted the man that saved his life above anyone, even if years passed without so much as a smile between them. In life, that kind of trust is hard to find and harder to maintain. It was one of Mints' greatest achievements. If the greatest feat the Devil ever managed was to convince the world he didn't exist, Anatoly Mints was Satan himself. And he was in the process of pulling off the biggest heist of his career to date.

"So, where is the key? Is it in this briefcase?" Mints asked and lifted the handle of the case.

Natalia was impassive. Mints grinned. He liked a challenge and Natalia knew how to give him one. He was a man with a small ego who sought gratification outside himself, from others, because he was too conscious of his rise from poverty. The feeling that he didn't belong. Too conscious that it could be snatched away at any time. He was like a street urchin with a bright red apple, cowering and snarling, afraid that people might take it away. That is what she read in him. And was what she used to her advantage.

The heavy doors creaked open again. The footman stepped back and two more people entered. A woman and a man, both dressed in the brown, military dress, working suits of the *Sluzhba vneshney razvedki Rossiyskoy Federatsii*. The Foreign Intelligence Service of the Russian Federation.

But, they didn't work for the Russian Federation. They worked for Anatoly Mints. A private foreign intelligence operation. Outside the control of the Russian State. Beholden, indirectly only, to Vladimir Putin himself. And controlled by Anatoly Mints. Natalia could see he was proud of having the woollen-suited ex-SVR officers goose stepping into his office in their high-shine riding boots. This was a man for whom Stalin was a god. A man with no parents, who thought the Russian state was his mother, and he was Stalin's seed.

"Hello, sir," the woman said. She had bobbed blonde hair under a side hat. She stood at ease at the corner of his desk.

"Matrona," Mints said in greeting. He called her by her formal title. Matron. She stooped towards him in a bow. When the Russian state decided to close the Kazan Sparrow School, and move away from state sponsored sex-as-espionage, Mints saw an opportunity. Just as he had when Russian state assets were sold at rock bottom prices and then flogged on the international markets at their true value. Mints saw an opportunity that no-one else saw. He, of all people, knew that information was power. And, the right information was powerful beyond measure.

He hired the instructors, recruited the spies, and rebuilt the school in the grounds of his own compound. Beholden personally only to him. He'd brought decades of Russian state-owned intelligence and know-how in-house. It made him one of the most powerful men inside Russia. He had files on everyone who mattered, and some on those who didn't.

Natalia was his best sparrow, even though she had so far resisted his advances. The other girls weren't so lucky, because they weren't as good, and they did what he wanted.

They earned their keep. Matron was his best instructor and in charge of the school.

The bald, thin man to Matron's right was Igor Agoranov. He had sunken eyes and his skin looked thin and veiny and pulled tight on his face. Mints called him *Kretin* behind his back. The dark rings under his eyes reminded him of a ghoul. He was a liaison between the SVR-proper and Mints' organisation, which he'd called *Smert' Predatelyam*. Death to Traitors. People called it Predator. Mints had recreated Stalin's Death to Spies in his own image.

Mints looked impatient. Sweat marks started to show on his tailored shirt. He removed his gold cufflinks and rolled up his sleeves. His forearms were hairy and he had sweat on his top lip.

"So, everyone is here, where is my key?"

Agoranov and Natalia looked to Matron. She swallowed, nervous, and said, "The mission was a success, sir. Natalia gained his confidence and incapacitated the British General, as you ordered. She took his assets, as intelligence suggested the code would be on his person or diplomatic possessions."

"But not the English assassin?" Mints said. "Why is he still alive?" His eyebrows were shoved together and his whole face seemed to compress. Natalia imagined him like a kettle about to whistle. She braced herself for him to boil over. Matron didn't respond. "Why is he still alive, do you have some sympathy with him?"

Matron looked away and continued.

"We also infiltrated his homestead and conducted a thorough search of the premises. The *resursy* didn't find the intelligence we were after."

Mints dried his lip with the back of his hand and said softly, "Well, where is it?"

Matron looked to Agoranov and then Natalia. Agoranov lifted his chin. He had a deep and loud voice for a slight man, and said, "Sir, my contacts in Foreign Intelligence tell me that there is significant activity from the British MI6. They have noted increased chatter and all British intelligence assets under their command have been stood up."

"For what purpose?" Mints asked and flicked some dust from his desk.

"We believe they are chasing a defecting asset. We aren't certain, but there is indication that the agent, Stirling Hunt, is on the run."

"Do they know about the code?" Mints asked.

"I do not believe so. The SVR are unsure and are trying to calculate why the need for such strong counter measures for one rogue agent, however, the true nature of the deception remains hidden from them."

"Make sure it stays that way. If they find out, I am going to know it was you Igor," Mints said and looked at Natalia. His stare felt like it cast a shadow over her. He lifted his index finger off the desk, "And you?" he said and pointed it at her.

"What about me?" She was defiant to the last.

"Did you screw him … our General?"

She could see the pleasure and the pain of the thought behind his cold black eyes. Did a dead man have something he could not? She wielded her control over him like a weapon. She chose not to respond to the provocation. Let him simmer. The kettle had finished boiling now, the water was hot enough already.

"I believe the General was smart. Stupid, like all men, who think with their *chleny*, but smart enough to know his own weakness and the power of the intelligence he is carrying."

"Spit it out, Natalia," Matron commanded.

"I believe the agent, Hunt, has what you seek."

"And where is he now?" Mints drummed an impatient finger on the desk.

"He has the entire British Secret Intelligence Service after him," Natalia said.

"Is that supposed to impress me?" Mints was indignant. "Bring him to me. Preferably alive. Dead is perfectly fine. Even though after all of the pain he has caused me in the past, I would prefer him dead. Bring him alive and I will finish the job Kabazanov was supposed to do all those years ago."

"Are you not worried this might end the same for you as it did for Kabazanov?" Natalia asked. Agoranov and Matron held their breath. Mints considered it.

"No," he said. He was in his fortress and had resources beyond what anyone else had at his disposal. He didn't seem concerned. Natalia wasn't sure he should feel so secure.

CHAPTER NINE

Who could he trust? Even sat there with the man of God, Hunt knew he couldn't trust him. He had no one to turn to. The more he thought about who he could contact, the more certain he was there was only one person.

The only people you can trust at a time like this; it's not your family, it's not your friends, and it's not your wife. It's the people you went into battle with. The brothers-in-arms who stood by your side knowing they were willing to lose their life for you, and that you would lay down your life for them. There was only one person Hunt trusted above all others.

"Here's the plan," Hunt said to the rabbi, "You're going to drive. It doesn't matter where. I'll lay down in the backseat under that blanket that you have and you just be a rabbi and go for a drive. If anybody stops us, you tell them, it's your favorite time of the year to take your beloved Jaguar on an open road, because the roads are empty and everybody is stuffed with turkey."

"You mean lie?" The rabbi contemplated.

"For the greater good, yes. But, first things first Rabbi. We need to shave your face."

The rabbi glanced at the shoulder holster and the grip of the pistol. He decided not to argue.

DRESSED, Hunt followed the rabbi out of the service door. He had his palm on his pistol, just in case. Under his arms he carried some of the rabbi's things. A hat, coat and blanket. The rabbi climbed into the front seat and Hunt lay down along the back seat and prepared the blanket to cover himself.

"All right Rabbi, you are doing a good thing here. Just head south until I tell you. You can follow signs for Gatwick Airport."

Gatwick was an international airport to the south of the city. Crucially, it was outside the main motorway that formed a ring around the city. If Hunt could get out of the wider cordon and outside the city limits, he knew he had a chance.

Hunt would've preferred to go alone. Less chance of something going wrong. But, this was the next best option. Even if there were roadblocks and they had his profile, a rabbi - with or without part of his beard - was an unlikely target for a stop.

Hunt knew though, with modern technology, they were more likely to be tracking his movement from a control centre using road traffic cameras, vehicle registration plates, and facial recognition software and getting matches automatically from the machine.

So, Hunt lay wedged between the back and front seats in the rabbi's car and tried not to look up. He needed to stay hidden from the silent eyes in the sky. His clothes were still damp, but they were warm, and he had the rabbi sweating in the front because Hunt asked him to turn the heating all the way up. Hunt had also made the rabbi put on one of his

73

heavy, long, rabbi's robes and wear a white prayer shawl. All part of the effect.

"I can't see a bloody thing with my hat over my eyes like this!" the rabbi complained.

Hunt had the middle console pushing him in the kidney, and he promised himself, then and there, first chance he got, he was buying the most expensive king size mattress he could afford and having hot showers every night for the rest of his life.

Hunt tried to relax and put the thoughts of the three hour drive to the back of his mind. He had to do a lot of planning to work out the next steps. And he planned to do his thinking while the rabbi was listening to Smooth Talk Radio and muttering to himself about how little he could see, and about how bad the rain was.

"CAN'T BLOODY SEE ANYTHING," the rabbi said.

"Rabbi! You potty mouth!" Hunt jested with him.

The rabbi said, "Oh, guff!" and waved him away. They sat quietly.

"Why are you going to Gatwick anyway. You flying somewhere?" the rabbi asked.

He played the role of the cab driver well. "Good guess, Rabbi," Hunt said, and moved position away from the hard plastic that had been sticking into his ribs for over an hour.

"No, I mean I know planes are flying from Gatwick, but my question is more about; did you think you will actually get onto a plane? Do these people that are chasing you know it is in your mind to try to get on an aircraft and fly away? Wouldn't they be looking for you?"

"I'm not flying anywhere Rabbi ... because, I think you're right they're all looking for me. You're going to do me a favour when we get there. You're going to go and meet somebody that I need to meet, in the arrivals hall, and bring them back to the car."

"What, you mean you're just going to let me loose in an international airport and hope that I don't speak to the authorities?"

"I did think about that," Hunt said, "And, two things occurred to me. Firstly, good luck trying to find somebody in an international airport to believe some crazy old man with a half-shaved beard who's walking free around the airport talking about being kidnapped. You'd sound mad. Second, I feel like you've grown attached to me during our time together, Rabbi," Hunt said with a grin. "Turns out I feel like I've grown attached to you too. And, I just don't think that you're the type of man to make a promise and then break it."

"Promise? What promise? When did I ever say a promise to you...?" The rabbi seemed shocked at the suggestion.

"You said you understand me, Rabbi. You said you 'don't agree, but you understand'. And if you understand, then you also understand that this is bigger than you or me. You have to understand that although from my appearance I look like somebody you can't trust, the reality is, if you don't trust me the world will shift on its axis. The lives we have now will never be the same, because whatever it is that the people who are after me want, there's no way they would be doing what they are doing unless it could change the world. Understand?"

"You sure about that?" the rabbi asked. "These people you trust, would they be chasing you if they trusted you?"

Hunt was quiet.

"You're right. I can't trust anyone right now. But, I am doing this for the right reasons. And, even if you never see it in the news, the decision you make in the next hour is going to be the most important decision you ever make. Something big is happening, Rabbi. Believe me."

The rabbi was quiet and drove on. He checked the

rearview mirror and finally said, "Okay. Okay, yes. I believe you."

"Yes, yes. I believe we are nearly here, so many cars ..." the rabbi said and peered out of the windscreen at the big blue boards overhanging the motorway. "I still think you're crazy for coming to a busy international airport, Mister No-one. But it's your own funeral, as they say in the movies, *ay?*"

All right, old man, time for action.

"Oh, *Meyn Gott!*" The rabbi said, "Have you seen these parking prices? I could buy a block of cheese for less than an hour at Gatwick."

"Never mind that, Rabbi. You're not gonna pay to park. Just follow the signs for the departure drop off and walk from there. It's free."

"But, if I leave the vehicle it'll be towed," the rabbi said. He was very concerned. The traffic was heavy. Christmas time was some of the busiest days for United Kingdom airports.

"Don't worry, it's not gonna get towed. I promise," Hunt said.

The rabbi did as he was told, and followed the signs for the drop off point. Hunt was going to let him park and head inside to check the boards for the arrival flights from Helsinki. He was sprightly, an older man, but a brisk walker. He had an open gait and waved his arms as he walked. It would still take him at least the ten minutes that they were allowed to park in the drop-off zone, before anybody took any interest. It was still risky. If he was going to get out of this, the next ten minutes were probably the most important of the whole escape.

Hunt's heart thumped in his chest and he concentrated intently. He wanted to make sure that they would be out of sight of any closed circuit television cameras. So, as they drove in, he cautiously raised his head, and checked the top of the street lights to see where there might be a blind spot.

"Just up ahead here, Rabbi. Do you see the car pulling out in front of the VW Transporter? Park in front of it and get as close as you can to his front. You do have parking sensors on this old Jag, don't you?"

"Parking sensors?" the rabbi said defiantly. "What do I need parking sensors for? You know how long I've been driving? Do you think I have any parking sensors in my life?"

As it turned out the Jag did have parking sensors. The rabbi was confident in his ability and while the taxi driver of the Transporter was helping his passengers unload their luggage, the rabbi parked the car mere inches from its front bumper. The rabbi harrumphed. He was proud.

Hunt climbed out of the back and into the front passenger seat. He rolled the blanket up again and inside it was the bundle of clothes that he'd brought from the rabbis office in the synagogue.

"Perfect parking," Hunt said. The rabbi was pleased. "Right, Rabbi, listen carefully. I am going to go into the terminal building and look for that friend of mine. I'll leave your keys in the toilets nearest to the check-in counters. Ten minutes after I've gone in, you get out of the car, and come in after me. Head straight for the toilets and your keys will be in the first stall in the men's room."

"But, I thought -"

"Change of plans, Rabbi. Only minor though. I go in first, you follow ..."

The rabbi nodded slowly. Hunt took the keys out of the ignition. The rabbi looked concerned.

"Don't worry about it," Hunt said when he saw the rabbi's expression. He dangled the keys, "You'll have these back in no time."

The rabbi nodded and looked at the steering wheel. Hunt

put his hand on the rabbi's shoulder, like a coach giving a pep talk to a player.

"What I need you to do now is, as casually as you can, follow me into the terminal building and find a board that will give you the arrival information. You're looking for all the arrival flights from Helsinki for the next few hours. Write them down. Then go into the men's toilets and get the keys."

The rabbi patted himself down and looked for a pen, which he found.

"And after?" the rabbi asked.

"And then, come back to the car. It shouldn't take you more than the ten minutes, which is exactly the amount of time we're allowed to stay parked here."

"And, how do I know you won't just take off?" the rabbi asked.

"Because I need the flight details you're getting for me ..."

"Before you go," the rabbi said, "Tell me, please. Are you not afraid?"

The rabbi looked across at Hunt. The rabbi had a look of pity on his face. Hunt was quiet. He thought for a moment. Was he scared? Not of dying. Certainly not. He didn't feel that kind of fear. He wasn't afraid of pain or hurt. The only thing he was afraid of was not succeeding. He still had a mission. Soames had still given him the mission of finding out what happened to General Patrick. And, Hunt still had a sense of duty, even if it was to the General and his family. Her Majesty still paid him her shilling, albeit into an offshore private bank in the Caymans. He had a duty to find out why - and who - had targeted the General and what they wanted. The thought of not succeeding was the only thing that gave him pause.

"No, I am not afraid, Rabbi. Someone, like you, once told me that some people were born to be warriors. I now know that is what I am, and what I am destined to do. So, I am not afraid of what the future holds. Only of losing."

The rabbi sighed and composed himself. Hunt opened the door, and just before he stepped out Hunt said, "Listen, Rabbi. One last thing ... please. It's really important ... if anything happens, if anything happens that makes you unhappy and that you really don't agree with, please, give me ten minutes. Just wait ten minutes before you tell anyone. Could you do that?"

The rabbi looked at the rain hitting Hunt's boots and trousers.

"Yes, okay. Last promise. I will give you the ten minutes."

Hunt stepped out into the rain and walked towards the airport building. He stood tall, shoulders back, and crossed the tarmac and walkway towards the departure lounge. Clumps of people rushed from parked cars and tried to get out of the rain. It was busy and that helped.

Hunt mingled in with them. He made sure to have his face clear and walked directly in front of the cameras. Like he wanted to be seen. He stood in front of the board for a moment, and made a mental note of where the cameras were. He waited for them to swivel.

In his mind, Hunt saw the entire departure hall from above, like a floor plan, and he imagined the angles of the cameras as they scanned. Hunt then moved tactically from position to position until he was sure that he was in a dead zone and not covered by any camera. He may as well have been invisible for those few seconds. When he was, he made his way to the nearest WCs.

He went into an empty disabled toilet and latched the door. His heart was racing, he only had moments, and set to work. He got undressed. And then unraveled the blanket. In it were the items he took from the synagogue.

Hunt put on one of the rabbi's wide brim hats. Next, he pulled on the rabbi's black robe. It was a bit tight, but it fit. Next, he put a white prayer scarf over his shoulders, and that just left one last thing to do.

Carefully, he reached into his coat pocket and pulled out the long, grey beard hairs that he'd cut from the rabbis face. It wasn't pretty. He created a facial covering, held together with string and sellotape. He attached the clear tape behind his ears and under the hat, so that from above, all you could see were long strands of beard. It would do the job for anybody using facial recognition on a grainy monitor. He pulled the hat down over his eyes so that it covered most of his face from the top angle, just like the rabbi had it on the drive, and would have it when he walked in.

Hunt checked his watch. He opened the disabled toilet door a crack and saw the rabbi heading towards the men's toilets. Hunt signalled to him and the rabbi approached him. Hunt opened the toilet door just wide enough for the rabbi to slip inside.

"I thought you said in the men's toilets," the rabbi said. As he turned, he saw Hunt dressed like him. Before he could say anything, and just as Hunt recognised the surprise on the rabbi's face, Hunt moved behind the rabbi and put him in a choke hold. It was quick and effective.

The rabbi struggled and gagged and he kicked out, but it was no use. It was like a boa constrictor squashing a mouse. The rabbi's body went limp. Hunt put him down gently on the toilet seat. He felt bad about it, but it needed to be done. He checked the rabbi's pulse. He was breathing. Hunt removed the hat from the rabbi's head, his scarf and took them. Once he was happy, he left the toilet, and used a coin to lock it from the outside. It now showed as engaged. A few more valuable minutes.

Hunt stooped and dropped his shoulders. He took on the characteristics of a much older man. He changed his gait and adopted the swinging arm action he'd noticed the rabbi made when he walked. Like an actor, he adopted the persona of the rabbi. He used all the willpower he had not to look up. Hunt left the terminal building and made a straight line for the waiting maroon Jaguar.

He noticed a luminous yellow high-visibility vest clad parking attendant punching numbers into his handheld device. Hunt did his best you Yiddish impression of the rabbi and said, "Good evening young sir, Merry Christmas to you, I trust this isn't a ticket for my vehicle here?"

"This your car?" the traffic attendant asked, knowing it was. "You can't be here for more than ten minutes. In fact, you aren't supposed to leave the vehicle at all ..."

"Yes, sir, forgive me. You see, it was my daughter's first trip abroad and I didn't want to leave her on her own. I'm terribly sorry if I've caused you any problems."

"Move the car right now and I won't have to issue you the fixed penalty notice."

"Yes sir, right away, sir. I'll get in the car now and hit the highway. I'm headed back to London ..."

Hunt climbed in the vehicle, started the maroon Jaguar, put the car into drive, and pushed his foot hard into the accelerator. The big car lurched and pulled out of the parking lot and Hunt sped off into the night and the rain. Now, he just needed the rabbi to give him those ten minutes he asked for.

CHAPTER TEN

Soames sat reclined with his back to his desk and looked into the night. He switched from chewing his cuticles to chewing the end of a pen. Holland burst into his office.

"He's at Gatwick," Holland said, out of breath.

Soames swivelled in his chair and stood in one movement. "Right now? You're telling me he's at Gatwick, right now? Let's go," Soames said.

Holland walked behind Soames and followed him into the operations room.

"We've got a break in this case people!" Soames said.

The level of activity in the operations room went up when they saw and heard Soames. A young, balding, analyst in round spectacles, stood in front of a presentation screen. On it was an image of Hunt walking into the departure building at Gatwick airport. It was frozen on him and he stared directly into the camera. Soames stood with his arms crossed and looked at it.

"When was this taken?" Soames asked.

"Thirty-seven minutes ago," the analyst said. "By our best estimate, he is still in the building."

"Estimate!?" Soames bellowed. There was a frenzy of

clacking on keyboards and people moving around. "Are we making estimations now, instead of having certainties? Do you people have any idea about the person we are going after here? If he is at Gatwick, I need to know."

"We don't deal in certainty, Director," Holland said. He spoke on behalf of the team of analysts. "You know better than anyone, sir, that we deal in probability, and deal in risk."

"Well, the risk is pretty damn high if he is probably at Gatwick. Wouldn't you agree, Mister Holland? And this intelligence is an hour old."

Holland stood silent. His face flushed. His suit jacket was open, he stood with one hand on his hip, and gestured towards the balding analyst with his other. "How did he get to Gatwick?"

"We're working on it, sir," another analyst sitting at a computer terminal said. Soames glared at her. She ducked her head and kept working.

"Well, find out goddamn it!" he bellowed again. "If he is there, and it's a big if, I need to get on the phone to MI5 and the Civil Aviation Authority and close the entire airport on one of the busiest nights of the year. So tonight, we're dealing in certainty, and not probability. Tell me for certain whether he is or isn't at that bloody airport!"

"I think I've got something!" the same female agent said.

"Put it up on the screen," Holland said.

Grainy black and white video footage showed on the screen. Car headlights shone at the camera and partially obstructed the view as they drove past. They were looking at the back of a Jaguar X-type. "Watch closely," the analyst said while looking at her screen. "Here the car comes, watch the back seat. Now!" she said. Just then, a head slowly raised into view in the back seat and scanned around the car. They could only see eyes and the forehead.

"That's him, that's Hunt," Holland said.

The car pulled in front of a black VW Transporter and

was lost from view. The camera angle flicked. The next video was Hunt walking towards the building, looking directly at the camera. Then inside the terminal building. "We lose him now," Holland said.

"Well, bloody well find him, don't try and tell me with the most sophisticated network of closed circuit cameras in the world our number one target escaped our view?"

Soames' blood pressure was up. He sweated. Holland tried to calm him. "We'll find him, sir," he said quietly and gave Soames a look that said 'reign it in'. Soames ignored him.

"Here goes the driver," the female analyst said. "He goes in, here."

"What's he, a rabbi?" Soames asked. His eyes darted over the screen. He looked confused.

"He enters the men's room, and then, a few minutes later, here he is again, leaving the terminal building. He gets in the car and drives away. Hunt is still in the terminal building somewhere."

"So, what is he doing ... Hunt, what are you doing?" Soames asked no-one in particular. "Is he flying somewhere, meeting someone? What's the plan here? Sneak aboard an aircraft with the key and disappear. Where is he going?"

"We don't know, sir."

"Yes, there is a hell-of-a-lot you don't know." Soames turned to the room. "Come on people! This is your chance to shine. Tell me who the hell that rabbi is. Tell me how he knows Hunt and what he was doing there. Give me information. We're on the clock. Give me all the footage we have from Gatwick, and give it to me now!"

"What about the rabbi?" Holland asked.

"Christ, Tom!" Soames said in frustration. He took a breath. He'd never felt so tense. "First, get an All-Ports Warning out. And, get a patrol car after him and stop. Search the car. Bring him in ..."

"Here?"

"No, not here. Nearest local station. Dress it up. A traffic violation. Send someone down and question him. Hunt is the priority."

"What about the airport, sir?"

Soames looked at the black and white footage on the screen. "You think he's there?"

"He didn't get back in the car," Holland said. "So where did he go? We've checked the surrounding cameras for him leaving on foot."

"And?"

"Nothing."

"Fine. Set a perimeter. Get onto aviation and tell them we need flights grounded. Don't forget, we trained him to fly. Make sure all private aircraft, helicopters and turboprops, are grounded. Say a drone is in the airspace and we need to clear it. That'll buy us some time. Send some of our guys to the departure lounge. Covert. No uniforms. I want it cordoned off. Concentrate our resources there. Search the place. In the meantime, confirm where the bloody hell he is. And do it fast," Soames said.

HUNT HEADED SOUTH and stayed on the country roads. He kept checking the rearview mirror and expected to see the flash of blue lights. He needed to swap vehicles again. These back roads were slippery, narrow and full of potholes. He passed through village after village and kept a lookout. As he approached a small village called Maplehurst, He saw a sign for the Whitehorse pub, Hunt slowed down and peered out through the bashing windscreen wipers and the sleet. Hunt craned his neck as he passed the white painted pub. The lights were off. It looked dark and lifeless. He slowed the Jaguar down and came to a stop. He did a three point turn and headed back towards the pub.

The parking lot was behind the public house, down a narrow driveway and around the back. It would be good cover and allow him to ditch the rabbi's car while out of sight of the street.

He pulled into the parking lot and switched off the engine and sat quietly and listened to the sound of rain on the car. He took a deep breath trying to calm his mind from thinking too much about what he had just done. He knew he needed to get out of the country. He was like a canned lion. It would be no challenge for the people hunting him. He had to get off the island.

Hunt stepped out of the Jaguar and put the keys on top of the rear tyre. At least once it got out of the police compound, the rabbi could have his precious car back. The rain made his hair stick to his forehead and Hunt blinked and squinted as the water dropped into his eyes. Soon, he found what he was looking for, a small, older car from the late-nineties or early-two thousands.

Something without an alarm and which he could start easily. He saw an old white hatchback. Something French and felt like his luck was finally turning. It was easy enough to get inside, but Hunt had to ratchet the seat all the way back, and the car was still too small for him. It didn't make him smile. He ripped off the plastic cover under the steering column and hot-wired the car. He knew it wouldn't be reported stolen until the morning.

CHAPTER ELEVEN

The English Channel was around twenty miles wide. Even with the currents, people swam it every year in under twenty hours. In fact the record was just over ten hours. Hunt wasn't planning on swimming it, but he was planning to cross it.

The Royal Navy Sailing Association was based in Gosport, near Portsmouth. Hunt knew it well. It was where he'd learned to sail. He also knew that at Christmas, on a night like this, the nearby Haslar Marina would be empty and unsecured.

He pulled into the car park near the marina. He ripped the registration plates off the hatchback and put them in a black rubbish bin. A tall, black fence ran around the outside of the Haslar Marina. Hunt stood on the edge of a two foot high brick flower bed close to the steel fence and grabbed onto the top of the fence posts. He could feel that the fence was slippery but he had the benefit of a tall coniferous tree overhanging the fence.

Rich people weren't concerned about yacht theft, it didn't seem. Hunt climbed on top of the fence and jumped down the other side and stayed in a crouched position and listened again. All he heard was the patter of rain and swishing of the branches. The wind was up, it meant a stormy sea.

Hunt walked around the back of the wooden hut near the fence and made his way down to the wooden jetties of the marina. The jetty creaked and bobbed in the swell. It was a miserable night. Like the car, he looked for something small, inconspicuous, and easy to sail by himself. He paced the jetties until he found what he was looking for. A beautiful, white and blue hulled Hallberg-Rassy 342.

She was sleek, she was good looking for a teenage boat, and she had a trustworthy Volvo diesel engine onboard. Hunt made ready for the crossing. The rain soaked him through as he unzipped her covers and stowed things away. He broke into the below deck and found a life jacket and some water-proof over-layers. The engine spluttered and fired and he kept her dead slow as he pulled her out of the marina and into the English Channel.

SOAMES STOOD and watched the monitors in the operations room. Holland was next to him. It was the nerve centre, in the basement, and set up specifically to catch one of their own. Commanders and analysts were all glued to the same screen. They watched a live camera feed from the lead field agent as his covert team searched the airport. The picture from the camera shook as the agents ran through the departure hall. Scared passengers jumped out of the way and the agents ran towards where Hunt had last been captured on closed circuit television. They got to the toilets. One of the agents grabbed a nearby man in a grey coverall who was mopping the floor. "The key, the key!" they yelled and grabbed him and pulled him towards the disabled toilet door. He fumbled with the key. The agents pulled out handguns and Soames could hear civilians in the background screaming. They pulled open the door and shouted in loud, authoritative voices trained to ensure compliance, "Get down on the ground! Get down on the ground! Hands above your head."

"Who is it," Soames demanded quietly. Holland, in radio communication with the lead agent said, "Alpha one, confirm the suspects identity."

The camera moved forward into the large toilet. The agent bent down and lifted the wide brimmed black hat off the suspect's head. He grabbed a handful of hair and twisted the suspect's face towards the camera. Soames and Holland were looking at a scared old man dressed as a rabbi.

"It's not him," the lead agent's voice came over the loud-speaker.

"No shit," Holland said, and then pressed the pestle to speak to the agent. "Roger. Copy Alpha One. Zero Alpha, out."

Soames cheeks were glowing red. His fists were clenched by his side. He wasn't breathing. Just staring at the screen.

FOR A SECOND, just after the first storm-sized swell hit the stern, Hunt thought about chucking the watch into the sea. Was it really worth it? It occurred to him that he could sail anywhere... then the second swell rocked the yacht and his mind was made up, before he was thrown overboard, he decided to find land as soon as possible.

That meant France. He pointed her north of Calais and held on tight as the sleek hull pounded into the dangerous sea.

Hunt was exhausted. It was the early hours of the morning and he could see lights twinkling from shore. The lights appeared and disappeared as the yacht rose and fell in the stormy seas. Hunt steered away from the lights and set the heading due west. He wanted open space away from prying eyes and inquisitive humans.

CHAPTER TWELVE

Exhausted, soaked through with salty sea water, feeling a deep, clammy cold that penetrated to his bones, Hunt waded ashore.

During his training as a Royal Marine, they'd recreated the D-Day landings. Full gear, soaked kit, chafed skin, dragging your boots out of the sandy mud and up the beach. He felt like that now. Except there was no warm brew at the end of this. Only more miles to run.

Hunt pulled at the cold steel chain attached to the yacht's anchor and planted it in the sand. He found a small boulder and placed it on top of the anchor. He wasn't sure why he'd bothered, but he also didn't want some stranger's yacht floating off into the middle of the Channel in rough seas. The rain lashed down and he wiped his face and slicked his hair back to stop the water dripping into his eyes.

In the near distance, to the north, he saw a huddle of people standing next to the water. Some others dragged an inflatable raft towards the sea. The huddle of people looked scared and cold and stood close together, like a waddle of penguins braced against an Antarctic storm. Hunt started walking towards them. His socks squelched in his wet boots.

One of the men dragging the raft, dropped it, and started towards Hunt. He waved his arms and shouted at him. As Hunt got closer he heard what he was saying, "Go away! Go away! We don't need you!"

Hunt put his hands up in submission and yelled to the man, "You speak English?"

"I speak English! I speak English. What do you want here?"

He was a short, round, Arab-looking man, with thick eyebrows, slitty eyes, and a hooked nose.

"Who are those people?" Hunt asked.

"Why do you care? They are not your people. Leave us alone. Do not come here ..." the man said.

Hunt was shivering cold and needed to get out of the wind in the rain. "Listen, I've just come across the sea and I nearly died. You can't send those people out there. You can't send those people out there in that raft. They will die."

"Yes, but you didn't die, did you? Insha'Allah."

"I'll tell you what," Hunt said. "Where is your boss? Where is the man who is in charge of sending those people, those refugees, across the Channel?"

"Why do you want to know? Do you think I am not the boss here? Leave us alone and go!"

The man waved his arms in Hunt's face and walked away back to the raft.

Hunt jogged slowly after him and turned him around, "Stop! Wait... Wait. Listen, listen. Maybe we got off on the wrong foot. I'm not trying to stop you from doing your job. I'm not trying to stop you making money. I just wanna talk to the guy who arranges everything. I have a deal for him."

Hunt pointed at the yacht bracing itself against the wind and leaning on its side.

"You see the boat? That's my boat. I've just sailed across the Channel. Let me talk to the man in charge. Maybe we can come up with a deal. Right?"

The fat Arab looked Hunt up and down, "What sort of deal?"

THE FAT ARAB led Hunt to a rusted minivan parked at the beach.

"Where are you taking me?" Hunt asked.

"Away from here. Get in... No questions."

Hunt wasn't going to argue about getting into a warm car and out of the rain. He did what he was told.

"If we see the cops, you know, the police, you must lie flat on the ground and not make any sound."

Hunt nodded, "Okay."

He wasn't sure where this fat Arab was from. He guessed Lebanon or Libya. Hunt spent time all over the Middle East. He knew the Iraqi people. He knew the Afghans, Iranians, and Kuwaitis. He knew the Saudis. He lived in Egypt when he was personally hunting al-Zawahiri. He spoke Arabic. But didn't want this round man to know he spoke Arabic.

Hunt sat in the back. The fat Arab turned the key and the engine made an attempt to turn over and then died. It sounded like a cassette recorder running out of battery. He turned it over again, and again, and finally the engine spluttered and made a low growl. It sounded sick. The exhaust was blowing. How they didn't get pulled over for roadworthiness, Hunt could never guess.

"Are those people going across?" Hunt asked, thinking of the waddle standing on the shore.

"No questions," the fat Arab said. There was a moment's silence. Then he said, "I don't think. Wind, no good. Rain, no good. Insha'Allah."

"And you don't have weather predictions, huh?" Hunt said and looked out the window. The Arab just glanced at him in the rearview mirror.

"You know the Jungle?" the fat Arab asked.

Hunt looked into the black eyes that stared back at him in the mirror. The man looked back at the road. Hunt knew 'the Jungle'. It was a notorious migrant camp built along the fence that led to the ferry terminal at the Port of Calais. Ten thousand African and Middle Eastern migrants and refugees lived in a squatter camp, each one desperate to cross the stretch of water in front of them and get to the shining light that was the United Kingdom.

"Is that where we're going?"

The Arab said nothing. He turned up the car radio and stared ahead.

———

THEY DROVE into a rundown area of Calais. The brakes squeaked every time he pressed the pedal. The tower blocks grew taller and the streets grew narrower. An old man with a walking-stick and flat cap glared at the driver, and then at Hunt as they passed him. The dirty looks got worse the deeper into the poorest part of Calais they went. There was graffiti and gang signs and slogans in green, red, and blue spray paint on all the buildings.

Hunt's sixth sense spiked. He was still wet and cold and tired. He knew he needed to have his wits about him. The driver eyed him shiftily the closer they got to their destination. Hunt was uncomfortable about it but he had no choice. No option but to trust a people-smuggling criminal from some bombed-out and overthrown dictatorship in north Africa. No option but to trust someone taking advantage of the hospitality and freedom in one of the world's oldest democracies to smuggle people. Someone who no doubt thought that because society was tolerant, it was soft. An easy target. Something to be taken advantage of.

The rattling old minivan pulled to the side of the road and

climbed the curb with a screeching wobble as it mounted the pavement.

"Here," the driver said and lifted his chin towards one of the buildings. "You follow me now."

Hunt climbed out of the back seat. The balconies on the buildings overhung, and looked down on him. Women hung washing and old men watched the street. The building Hunt stood in front of looked like it was about to collapse.

The fat Arab pushed his way into a communal entrance. It was a block of flats. The light in the entrance hall was out and others flickered down the corridor. It was damp, dingy and, Hunt was sure, infested with rats. The walls were painted lime green, it was all faded and peeling. The same spray-painted markings were at the top of each floor as they climbed.

Hunt was sure they marked the territory of the various criminal gangs. He balled up a fist and covered his mouth and coughed a wet cough. The fat man looked at him concerned at the sound. Hunt looked at his pale-white hands and blue-hued knuckle. Signs of hypothermia. The fat Arab slowed as he climbed. He wheezed and pressed his hands on his knees as he went up the stairs.

"To the top," he said and looked back. He was sweaty and gave Hunt an apologetic smile. "The stairs, they killed me ..."

When they got to the top, the Arab put his hands on his hips, and took a few deep breaths. Hunt waited. The Arab lifted a single index finger to indicate that he needed a moment. When he'd caught his breath he walked down the corridor and indicated for Hunt to follow him. He pushed his way into an apartment on the top floor and walked in.

Hunt could see several people sitting at a kitchen table. They were playing cards. Two men and one woman, listening to music, drinking tea, and smoking. The kitchen was cramped and what he would've expected from a social housing flat. It doubled as a dining room. They had the usual pots and pans and condiments out and a block of wood filled with knives.

Behind them, in the living room, was a younger, thinner Arab, with slicked over black hair and a well manicured goatee. He wore gold-rimmed sunglasses and held a large mobile phone to his ear. When the people at the table saw the fat Arab they smiled and greeted him. They were in the middle of an argument about the card game and giving one of the guys a hard time.

Hunt walked in behind the fat Arab. When they saw him they stopped talking and sat back a bit shocked. The woman at the table jumped up and pointed an accusing finger at the fat man. She wore a black hijab that covered her hair, not her face.

The fat man held his hands up defensively and spoke expressively and rapidly in Arabic, trying to set them at ease. The woman started yelling, Hunt couldn't place her accent. She was speaking in a type of local dialect. He could tell she wasn't happy though.

She went over to the guy sitting on the sofa and started giving him a hard time. The guy hung up and stood and came over to the kitchen table. The fat man started explaining what Hunt was doing there. A proposition. Hunt just stood in the middle of the kitchen dripping water on the floor and trying to stay conscious. The fat man was losing control of the situation and Hunt's condition wasn't helping.

"Listen, listen..." Hunt said and put his hands up in front of him to try and calm the situation. He wasn't sure if he was slurring or not. Hunt looked at the fat man, "Do they speak English?"

The fat man nodded, "Yes."

"Who's in charge here?" Hunt asked.

Nobody said anything. Everybody was impassive. The tension rose like a high-pitched whine on a violin. Hunt's tinnitus was playing up again. The sea water in his ear wasn't helping. Hunt looked at the younger Arab standing behind the table.

"Are you wearing your shades inside so people think you're cool?" Hunt asked. "I can't see if you're looking at me or not ..."

The younger Arab used the tip of his finger to slide his purple-lensed glasses down the bridge of his nose.

"See? I'm looking right at you. Do you have something to say to me? Say it. Or, get out."

So, you're the boss, Hunt thought.

CHAPTER THIRTEEN

"I need to get south, to Marseilles," Hunt said.

"So take the bus," the younger Arab said. He was deadpan, body language aggressive. He meant to be threatening. Hunt was feeling weary and easily provoked.

"I need to get to Marseilles, unseen ..." Hunt said and emphasised the final word.

"Search him," the young Arab lifted his chin and said to his friend sitting at the table. The colleague stood, slowly, all the while looking Hunt in the eyes. He pushed his chair back with his legs and came towards him. Hunt raised his arms. The colleague, a curly haired Arab man, patted him down. He had a look of immediate surprise and reached into Hunt's coat and pulled out his 9mm handgun. The curly haired one was even more aggressive and he waved the handgun in Hunt's face and screamed at him. Hunt lowered his head and moved his arms gradually closer to his centre in case he had to fend off any blows.

"Okay, okay ..." the young Arab in the sunglasses said and called off his attack dog. The curly-haired man glared at Hunt. Hunt could smell the tea and cigarettes on his breath. He stepped back, a smug look on his face, and sat back down at the table. He placed the handgun in front of him and glared at Hunt. He left the pistol there, in easy reach, menacingly close should Hunt try anything.

"Please guys, I just need a ride. Believe me. I don't want any trouble. I'm cold, I'm hungry, and I'm wet, and I just need a ride to Marseilles."

"We're not a taxi service!" the woman yelled.

The younger Arab looked at the fat man and jabbered in Arabic. He wasn't happy about this fat man bringing Hunt to the apartment. The fat man waved his arms and tried to defend himself by saying he tried to call, and that the young Arab was busy and didn't respond, then he turned to Hunt and said, "Tell him about the boat..." and then looked back at the younger Arab, "Listen."

Everyone around the table waited. Hunt saw the woman move towards the sofa at the back of the living room. Her hand dangled. She tried to look casual. Hunt knew it was always the quiet ones you had to worry about. In a group, the ones in your face, shouting and being aggressive, weren't the ones to throw the punches. It's the quiet ones at the back stalking around in the shadows riling themselves up without making any sounds or drawing any attention to themselves.

Hunt knew because that's how he was, unlikely to start a fight. Definitely the one who'd end it. He got the sense that the woman in the hijab was the one he had to worry about.

"There's a yacht anchored near where you were launching from on the beach. You can have it," Hunt said, "If you get me to Marseilles."

"And what do I want with some yacht?" the young guys said.

"Look at you," Hunt lifted his hand towards him, "You're a playboy. You could use it to complete the look. All playboys have a yacht," Hunt said.

His tongue was firmly in his cheek. He managed to get a

chuckle out of the guys at the table and they glanced at the younger Arab in the sunglasses.

"Or, you could sell it, or use it to transport those immigrants in something other than an inflatable raft ... Some of them might actually get to the country that they paid you to get to ... and not die drowning in a freezing cold sea." Wrong thing to say. This time there were no laughs. The table turned to look at their boss. The high-pitched grinding of the violin grew louder in Hunt's ear. It made him want to tilt his head to the side and bang it with his hand to get the water out. Instead, he just stood there. The fat man tried to say something and the young Arab held up his hand to silence him. Hunt was losing the room and he knew it. Time to push his chips all-in.

"The other card I have to play," Hunt said, "Is that unless you take the deal, I will make a phone call and have the French border force here in fifteen minutes."

The Arab in the sunglasses smiled a thin, confident smile for the first time. He touched the side of his gold-rimmed sunglasses and said, "Mister, if you could go to the police, you wouldn't be in my kitchen asking me for a journey..."

Bluff called. The air in the room all of a sudden felt very heavy. It was quiet. You could hear the traffic on the road far below and some kids kicking a football down in the street. Hunt's mind strayed to where he was aware of his wet clothes, how cold he was, and the way his trousers clung to his thigh.

"I guess your only option then is to kill me ..." Hunt said. No one moved. No one breathed. The fat man raised his hand and coughed. As he lifted it the curly-haired one at the table twitched and went for the gun. Hunt spun and in one movement he grabbed a carving knife from the block of wood, turned, and thrust down. It slammed into the back of the guy's hand. The curly-haired Arab screamed. Hunt grabbed the handle of the Sig Sauer before anyone else could react. Everything seemed to slow down. Hunt raised himself upright and fired a single shot between the eyes of the young Arab in the sunglasses. His head snapped back and his body crumpled to the floor. The woman screamed a vicious hate-filled scream and reached behind the sofa. She lifted an AK-47. Suddenly everything sped up. The automatic rifle was going to do enormous damage in the small flat. The way she raised it, and how insane with anger she was, there was no telling where the bullets would go.

Hunt flipped the kitchen table and dove to the floor. The fat man turned to run. The hammer on the AK-47 shot forward and the rounds punctured the table. Hunt stuck out a leg and tripped the fat man as he ran. The fat Arab went down hard and winded himself. The sound from the rifle firing reverberated around the small concrete apartment. The grating whine in Hunt's ears intensified. Wood chips and pieces of ceiling fell onto Hunt and the fat Arab. All the while the woman in the hijab was screaming at the top of her lungs. With every 7.62mm round fired the barrel of the automatic rifle lifted higher. Hunt took his chance. He rolled to his left and leaned around the table. He looked down the sight and lined up the three white dots against her knee. He fired and she screamed and her leg buckled under her. He still looked down the sight. She collapsed to the floor and tried to bring the rifle around to aim at him. The dots on the sight lined up with her forehead and Hunt squeezed again. He double tapped the trigger and there was a blip of red between her eyes and her head lolled to the side. The soles of the fat man's shoes squeezed as he kicked out like a newly hatched turtle headed for the sea. The last man back-pedalled. His eyes darted around. He was afraid and took quick deep breaths. He lunged for the AK-47 and Hunt squeezed the trigger again. The body slumped.

Hunt rolled onto his back and lay there looking at the ceiling. Damn it. Damn it to hell. The fat man was still swimming for the door, panting, and making an arse of himself. Hunt got up and grabbed the fat man by the scruff of the neck. Greedy fat bastard, he thought as he tried to lift him. Hunt dragged him past the bodies and pushed him down onto the sofa. The fat man whimpered. Hunt made his pistol safe. He got the fat man to crawl around on the floor and collect up all of the 9mm shell casings. And he did. He crawled around on his hands and knees whimpering as he collected the brass. Hunt knew he only had minutes.

"Right. Get up," Hunt said. "Take off your clothes ..."

The fat man stood up, but he was confused. Hunt looked at the gun in his hand and raised it.

"Take off your clothes."

The fat man danced on one leg as he removed his shoes and nearly fell as he took his trousers off. When he was undressed he threw his clothes onto the sofa. He stood there in his tight white underpants. Hunt planned to put the fat man's clothes on, at least they were dry, but when he lifted the shirt and gave it a sniff, he changed his mind.

"Please, please. I ... I can pay you, I have money. I know where money is. Please, please don't kill me. I pay. I pay," the fat man said.

Hunt lowered the handgun. His priority was to get some dry clothes on and get out of the apartment block before the French police arrived.

"Okay, okay," the fat Arab said and looked like a kid in a sweetshop. He was excited and nervous and glanced around. "In the bedroom," he said to Hunt.

Hunt flicked the gun and the fat man turned and went into one of the bedrooms. Hunt followed. The room was a complete mess. Clothes strewn about, DVDs lying on the floor. A mess. The fat man knelt at one of the cupboards and moved some clothes. There was an electronic combination safe on the floor. He tried the code and the machine beeped and gave him a warning. He stopped and looked at Hunt and gave a slight chuckle and tried the code again. This time the mechanism released and the safe unlocked. The fat man reached in and grabbed handfuls of Euros and held them up for Hunt.

"You see it? You see? I pay you. You go ..."

Hunt pushed the fat man so he rolled onto his backside and he stuffed the rolled up notes into his coat pocket.

Just then, Hunt heard a low cry. It sounded like it was in the next room. Definitely coming from inside the flat. Hunt looked at the fat man in his underpants sitting on his butt on the floor. The fat man's face looked panicked. That made Hunt curious. The fat man started jabbering about a job or something else to buy his life, but Hunt wasn't interested. He left the safe open and told the fat man to stand.

"Show me..." Hunt said.

The fat man was still trying to talk, trying to say something to explain his way out of it. The fat man led him to a door in the small passage. The door to the other room was locked. Hunt pushed the fat man out of the way and put his boot through the handle. The door crashed open and Hunt went in with his weapon raised. What he saw shocked him.

A young girl, wrists tied with leather straps to the bed posts. She had bobbed brown hair, and bruises on the left side of her face around her eyes and her lips were puffed up. She had a dish cloth pulled tight and tied around her mouth to muzzle her. She was only in her panties and her young body twisted and she started to sob at the sight of the gun.

Hunt turned back to the fat man. The rage inside of him was immediate and unforgiving. He couldn't remain calm. He shouted at the fat man like he was a dog that had pissed on his carpet.

"What is this!? What is this!?" Hunt yelled and gestured towards the girl.

"I don't know! Please. I don't know! I just work. I just do what they say. Not me! Not me."

"Stay here," Hunt said and the fat man cowered. Hunt went over to the girl. He crouched down. She was afraid.

"Shhh. Shhh," he soothed her. "I'm not going to hurt you. I'm here to save you. You're going to be okay," Hunt said and gently removed the dishrag from around her mouth.

"These people hurt you," Hunt said. The girl nodded, her eyes wet with tears, they ran down her cheeks. Hunt motioned with the handgun in his left hand, the fat man cowered in front of the built in wardrobes. Hunt couldn't abide men like this, men taking what wasn't theirs to take. Innocence.

"Did he hurt you?" Hunt asked and pointed the gun at the covering Arab.

The girl looked Hunt in the eyes. The fat man pleaded with his eyes, snot came out of his nose, and saliva dribbled from his mouth. She glanced at the fat man and gave a single nod and bit her lip.

There was a still moment in time. Hunt looked at the girl. He could see the fat man in his peripheral vision. Hunt pressed the trigger. And then kept on pressing it. The girl turned away and squealed at the sound. Hunt fired and fired until the action clicked. The rounds smashed into the fat man's body one after another and he collapsed to the floor.

"I'm going to look after you …" Hunt said. He untied her, dressed her in a robe, and carried her out of the flat. It was still early. The streets were quiet and the wetness and greyness kept the people wrapped in their beds. He put her gently in the back seat of the fat man's van. He didn't know what he was going to do with her. He just knew he was going to get her to safety. The old engine struggled to turn over as Hunt twisted the key. He swore. And tried again. It started. They headed out of town and to the south.

CHAPTER FOURTEEN

The phone on Soames' bedside table rang. He groaned and rolled over, turned on the light, and checked the time. It was almost two in the morning.

He picked up the receiver and rubbed his eye with his palm and said, "Hello?"

"We have a break in the case, sir," Holland said down the line. "We found —"

"Wait," Soames said, "I will be right down."

He hung up and climbed out of bed. He wanted to be there for this.

SOAMES WALKED into the basement operations centre. It smelled of bad breath, body odour and coffee. Sleep deprived analysts with pale skin and oily hair sat at their terminals and worked.

Holland stood in front of the screens. An obscured black and white closed circuit still image of a man behind the wheel was up. Soames strode up and stood next to Holland who half-turned. He went on without the formalities or small talk.

"We picked up some chatter on the wires, French police found an apartment full of dead Libyans. We believe that is their car," Holland said and pointed at the image on screen.

"That's meant to be him?"

"We believe so ..."

Soames went closer and peered at the image and grunted.

"We also have a report of a yacht stolen from Gosport. No sign of the vessel, but we're tracking the shipping lane channels in case of any sightings of an unmanned craft."

"Sounds thin, Tom," Soames said and turned from the screen. The analysts' eyes diverted quickly back to their screens. Soames looked at the lanky flunky in front of him and asked, "What makes you think it's him?"

"It has Hunt's *modus operandi* all over it."

"How, and more importantly, why?"

Holland opened his mouth. Soames continued, "Where is he going? What is he doing?"

"That we don't know yet but, we have a lead. That is a French traffic camera showing Hunt heading south on the A-twenty-six from Calais."

"So, he steals a boat. Kills a family. Steals their car ... and then, what comes next?"

"I've contacted the Interior Ministry, sir. To make them aware. We might need their support."

Soames was silent. He clenched his teeth and balled his hands up into fists. He was seething.

That should have been his call. How was this junior making decisions without him? Now, the whole world and their dog would know that they couldn't handle their own business and, worse, that there was something or someone worth chasing down. Now they had competition.

"I had to," Holland implored and checked over his shoulder at the prying eyes of the analysts.

"Oh, don't worry about them," Soames said and waved Holland's concerns away. Then said louder, "There's not a real tracker among them." Soames looked at the clock not the wall, "How long have you had now, thirty-six hours? And this is all you've got?" He gestured at the screen.

Soames looked back at Holland.

"Where's he going?"

Holland was silent.

"Or, maybe the better question is, where is he? He's undoubtedly there by now."

Soames and Holland stood and looked at one another silently. It was an unspoken truce. Soames took a breath. "Where is the car?"

"We haven't been able to locate it."

Soames rubbed his chin. His eyes searched Holland's face and then narrowed.

"France?" Soames said. "If he was traversing it, would he be heading south?"

Holland shook his head. "No."

"So, he is meeting someone in France ..." Soames turned back to the screen. "France," he said again. He dropped his hand and snapped his fingers and turned back to Holland. "What was his name? The chap Hunt did the mission in the mountains with?"

Holland's eyes widened as he said, "I think I know where he is going."

"Find him," Soames said. "And do it fast."

CHAPTER FIFTEEN

It was before dawn. Hunt pulled into a parking lot outside the *Commandement Légion Étrangère*, the French Foreign Legion Command in Aubagne, near Marseille. Hunt had driven all night. He'd kept to the speed limits and only stopped to drop the girl off at a hospital, made sure she was safe, and went on his way. He'd swapped the licence plates with a similar looking vehicle in a secluded *aire de service*. In France there are private campsites on the side of roads and in small towns. He made good use of one. A wash, shave, and change of clothes.

No doubt the French police would have found the apart-ment and the dead bodies by now. He wanted to be as far away from Calais as possible, besides, he was looking for someone. Someone he knew a long time ago. Someone he suspected he could trust. There weren't many of those in the world. He just didn't know exactly where he was. He knew he would be close though. He would have to wait until the recruitment office opened. He put his head on the car's window and tried to sleep.

A HEAVY TAP made him jolt and think that the window might break. Metal on glass. Hunt sat up. The sun was up. A uniformed Legion soldier in white *kepi* stood outside the car and glared in.

"Wake up!" he said in French. "You can't sleep here."

Hunt opened the door and the soldier stepped back.

"*Bonjour*," Hunt said. "Recruitment?"

"Ah, *oui*," the soldier said and looked him up and down. Hunt stretched. The soldier pointed at a building with a red-tiled roof, behind a white brick wall, topped with a green mesh fence that ran all the way around it.

Hunt walked across the tarred parking lot and climbed the stone stairs to the French Foreign Legion recruitment office. A sign said to wait, so he waited. He stood at ease and took a moment to take in the view. The clear early morning sun glanced off the wisp of cloud. It was bright and blue. Hunt looked up at a tall cone shaped cypress tree on the front lawn of the recruitment centre. It was still. The door opened and he snapped back from his daydream.

"You there!"

Hunt turned to see the recruitment corporal beckon him in. He was shown into a room and told to sit. It reminded him of a doctor's waiting room. Instead of posters of happy elderly people being wheeled out of hospital, like in a doctor's waiting room, there were posters of young men, chins up, with the regulation two millimetre haircut. They stood to attention under their Legionnaire kepi blancs. The famous white hats of the Foreign Legion. It was just like the recruitment centre he'd stepped into in Holborn all those years ago.

A recruiting sergeant came out of his office and stood in the doorway. He addressed Hunt with his eyes, his displeasure was clear, and after a moment, ushered him into the office. Hunt sat at the desk. The sergeant leaned back in his chair and clasped his hands and rested them on his stomach.

"Why do you want to join the Legion?" the sergeant asked.

It was a good question. The sergeant asked it about twelve times every day. Thousands of times a year. And he'd heard it all. Everything from 'on the run from the police', to 'want to learn French'. No-one ever said to die for a country that wasn't even theirs.

"I don't," Hunt said.

Silence. They sat staring at one another. The sergeant dropped his bottom lip and gave a small nod and sat forward. He put his hand out and said, "Passport."

"I don't have a passport."

The sergeant picked up a pen and pulled a piece of paper in front of him. He held the pen ready to write.

"You are illegal in France. Name?"

The sergeant had a heavy French accent, but Hunt doubted he was originally from France. Eastern Europe, he guessed. Probably Croatia or Czech.

"I don't have a name."

The interviewer gave his colleague a look. He checked his watch. Too early for this much trouble. He hovered a hand over the form he was required to fill in.

"*Uh-ha*. And what was your crime?"

"I've committed no crime."

He glanced up at Hunt and put the pen down.

"You know, you people, coming here and thinking even in the Legion we will simply accept the scraps of society," he caught himself and pressed his lips together. "Anyway, you look too old to join. Leave my office."

Hunt reached into his pocket and pulled out a silver coin. It was single sided. And, in the middle, it had a picture of the Legion emblem. Across the top it said 'Afghanistan'. It was a calling card, a promissory note. Whoever carried one was owed one favour by the brothers of the Legion. Owed a debt. Hunt had come to collect.

He slid it across the desk. The recruitment sergeant and his corporal looked at one another again. The sergeant picked it up and inspected it, placed it back on the desk, and raised his hand to his mouth. He leaned forward on his elbows.

"All right. Speak your request ..." he said.

"I need to find someone," Hunt said. "The man who gave me this," and pointed to the coin. "His name, when he was serving, was Philipe Lambert. A *Capitaine*. He was in the first *Régiment Étranger de Cavalerie*. The first Foreign Cavalry Regiment."

"The only Foreign Cavalry Regiment, now," the sergeant said bitterly.

The sergeant handed the coin to his corporal. "What did you say, the name?" he asked.

"Lambert," Hunt said.

The sergeant nodded to the corporal and he took the coin and left the room. As he left Hunt turned and called out, "No phone calls! Please ... don't phone anybody. This must remain private."

The corporal nodded and went out.

"He retired, injured," Hunt said.

"Okay," the sergeant said, "We will find him. No problems." He leaned back in his chair again while Hunt drummed his fingers on his knees and waited.

The corporal came back with a file. Hunt turned to him as he said, "I believe he is living on one of the *Légion Etrangère* vineyards."

The sergeant sat forward and studied the file. After a few anxious moments enduring the sergeant moving his lips to read and nodding occasionally, he clapped his hands and said, "*Voilà!* We have him."

He spoke rapidly in French to his colleague. He gestured at Hunt and back at the corporal and dropped his lower lip. The corporal beckoned to him and Hunt followed.

CHAPTER SIXTEEN

Hunt sat in the back of a camouflaged Arquus Trapper VT4 SUV, a French version of a military pick-up truck, and let the warm air of southern France rush over his face.

The recruiting corporal sat in front with the duty driver and they headed north. The Foreign Legion, *Légion Etrangère*, were the only regiment in the French military to have their own vineyard.

After about an hour driving through Provence they pulled up outside the white arch that said, *l'Institution des Invalides de la Légion Étrangère*, the gated entrance was painted at a slant in green and red, the colours of the Legion. One of the reasons Hunt was here, one of the reasons he had the promissory coin, was because of the Legion motto: *Tu n'abandonnes jamais les tiens, ni au combat, ni dans la vie*. You never abandon your own, in combat nor in life. He hadn't abandoned Lambert in the mountains and so Lambert wouldn't abandon him.

Hunt climbed out at the gates of *Domaine du Capitaine Danjou*. A full colonel with a row of medals across his breast and wearing military dress came out to meet the vehicle. The corporal threw up a rigid salute and held it, chin up, chest out, as he explained to the colonel what they were doing there. Hunt stood to the side and tried not to appear too mute or too out of place.

He failed.

The colonel nodded as the corporal spoke and looked Hunt up and down out of the corners of his eyes. The colonel was a large man, with big hands, and a round, welcoming face. Formalities complete, the colonel walked up to Hunt with an outstretched hand, and welcomed him to the vineyard.

"You are looking for Lambert?" he asked as they walked.

Hunt nodded, 'yes'. The colonel gave him the tour as they walked and talked Hunt through every one of his medals as they moved past row upon row of bare vines. Soldiers with long grey beards and some with prosthetic limbs tended the soil and tidied the vines.

" ... And this one, the *Légion d'Honneur*, this the National Order of Merit, this the Cross of Military Valour," he said proudly. Hunt was impressed, but eager to find Lambert. "You are an adventurer, like me?" enquired Colonel Normandy.

"I think so, yes," Hunt said. "Only with fewer medals."

"The medals are only for show," the colonel smiled. He stopped Hunt with his arm and he looked at him. "It is only here, that counts," he said and thumped himself in the chest. Hunt agreed. He thought the old colonel might be a touch mad. These types of places were for men with physical damage, but also societal issues.

"There is not much work in the vineyard in winter," Colonel Normandy said. "The soldiers are starting the pruning processes now. We work everyday, for those that are here with no family. No-one here is one with a family, but you are welcome to join ours. Up there," the colonel said and pointed to a bench and wooden table on a small rise over-looking the vineyard.

A group of men sat at the table and shared a coffee and a cigarette. Hunt thought Lambert must be among them. He started walking and the colonel left him to walk alone. The scene was idyllic. Hunt looked up at the limestone sides of Mont Sainte-Victoire as he walked.

He saw a head bob and then it looked up from the table at him, and then the person stood. It was Lambert. He took off the dark glasses and put them on the table and stepped out of the bench. He started towards Hunt at a brisk walk which turned into a jog and then a run. Hunt couldn't help but smile. He hadn't seen a friendly face in what seemed like years. When Lambert got within ten feet of him he stopped and stared. He looked at Hunt like he was seeing his long lost brother. Hunt put his hand out and Lambert walked up and hugged him tightly around the neck. They both laughed.

"*Merde! Espèce de foutu sauvage. L'assassin anglais est de retour,*" Lambert said with his hands on Hunt's shoulders. He called over to his mates sitting at the table. "This is the English savage!"

"You've been telling stories about me again?"

"All the time, my friend. All the time."

They walked to the table and Lambert introduced him. Hunt was offered some coffee from a thermos and he took it gladly. It was sweet and hot. He was offered a cigarette and he took that too. After they'd spent some time catching up and swapping stories, Hunt made a serious face that said, 'we need to talk'.

"So, what's up?" Lambert said in English.

Hunt cocked his head at the others sat around the table. Lambert creased his brow and said, "Don't worry, they don't speak *Anglais*.

"Brother, I need your help," Hunt said and immediately regretted having asked as he looked at Lambert's scarred eyebrows and eyelids. Lambert felt self-conscious and lifted the blackout sunglasses from the table and put them back on.

He still had vision out of one eye and he showed his prefer-
ence for the dominant one by looking at Hunt by turning his
head to see more clearly out of it. Hunt slid the one sided
silver coin across the table. Lambert picked it up and smiled
and closed his fist around it.

"Anything," Lambert said. "You need money, a place to
stay?"

"I need information ..."

"Okay, what sort?"

"I'm on the run, mate. I got mixed up in something very
big and very serious. I need someone who can get information from Secret Intelligence."

"CIA, MI-6?"

Hunt nodded.

Lambert gave a low whistle. He took the sunglasses off
and eyed up the guys at the table. They got the message and
stood up. They said their farewells to Hunt and made their
way back into the fields. Hunt watched as they blew warm
breath into their hands and rubbed them together against the
chill.

"Do you know someone who can get me a passport?"

"Big trouble, eh?"

"The worst kind ..."

Just then Hunt heard shouting from the field. It sounded
panicked. Hunt turned and saw a man waving his arms and
yelling as he ran. Lambert stood.

"We must go," he said. Hunt didn't react and Lambert
grabbed him by the lapel and pulled him up and said, "We
must go idiot! You've brought the police with you."

Hunt jumped to his feet. The pensive tranquility was
over.

"Come, this way ..." Lambert said and beckoned. Hunt
looked back and saw clusters of retired soldiers moving
towards the gates.

"Don't worry," Lambert said, "This farm is our country

now. The Legionnaires will defend it as if it were France. They will not enter easily. The colonel will not allow it, but we must go ..."

CHAPTER SEVENTEEN

THE CLUBHOUSE, LONDON

Rishi, one of the analysts, hung up the phone as the live feed on the screens flickered to life. "We have the feed from the satellite while it's in range," the analyst said.

"How long?" Holland asked.

"Around thirty minutes," Rishi said.

"Okay, concentrate," Soames said. " This will be over in ten. We have him now. Don't let him get away."

Soames and Holland were staring at the monitors. There was real time satellite feed looking down on the *Domaine du Capitaine Danjou* vineyard in Provence. The satellite zoomed out and showed gendarmes crowded outside the gate. On the other side, a huddle of retired Legionnaires armed with pitchforks and spades. There were blue flashing lights.

"Scan up," Soames said. "I want to see that traitor."

The image moved, over the vines in the field and towards

two men running in the opposite direction to the gate. Hunt, at the back of the pair, stumbled.

"There," Holland pointed. "That's them. That's Hunt."

"Stay on him," Soames said, and then under his breath, "Got you, bastard son of a bitch."

The satellite zoomed in. The operations room could see their shadows moving across the ground.

"They're headed for the trees! Tell the commander on the ground. Get some men on the other side of the wall."

"On it!" one of the analysts confirmed.

"We're going to lose visuals under those trees ..." Holland said.

"They can't get far," Soames said. "Tell them to get some men into the forest and cut them off. They're blocked by mountains north and south. We'll funnel them in. They're on foot. They can't get out of the cordon now."

A few minutes after the message was relayed, Soames watched as a team of black-clad assault gendarmerie started moving in close single line formation up the eastern wall. They were going to cut Hunt and Lambert off at the top.

PROVENCE, FRANCE

HUNT CAUGHT himself as he stumbled and managed to outrun the momentum.

"Come on!" Lambert yelled back at him. "The *gendarmes* are on the gate."

The local paramilitaries were trying to get into the compound. They were after him, no doubt about it. How did they find him? Had to be a tip off. Hunt felt the panic set in at the back of his throat again. No rest. No escape. He needed to get out of there. He ran hard to catch-up to Lambert. His body ached and he was tired.

"I know a way out," Lambert said in between breaths as they ran. They were headed for a forested part of the estate at the far end of the property. There was a high stone wall that ran around the entirety of the estate. Hunt knew if they climbed it they'd be spotted immediately. Lambert was leading them into a dead-end. He felt it was a trap.

"There's no way out from here," Hunt said.

"Trust me, come on. Hurry."

As they ran up, Hunt saw the overhanging branches that threw shade over that part of the vineyard. They got out of the sun and into the cool darkness of the shade.

"Over there," Lambert said and pointed at a pile of stones. They ran up and Hunt saw it was a well.

"It's dry, climb down."

Hunt peered over the edge. It was dark and cramped. He looked back over his shoulder at the gate. There was commotion, but he couldn't make out what was going on.

"You must make yourself small, thin, like this," Lambert said and raised his hands above his head like he was about to dive into a swimming pool. "Then use your legs and elbows to slow your fall. I will meet you at the bottom. You must hurry! If the gendarmes start to shoot, the others will not hold them for long."

Hunt heard a *clang* of metal on metal. *Clang. Clang. Clang.*

"They're trying to break through the gate. We must go now," Lambert said and pushed Hunt towards the well. "This is an escape," Lambert tried to reassure him. "One thing about the people here, they are as paranoid as they are crazy. No Legionnaire would rest here, unless there was a way out. A route out. The ones from Indochina built tunnels around this place many years ago. Now we can use them for what they were intended."

119

Hunt didn't need any more convincing. If a bunch of shell shocked and disabled soldiers from the first Indochina war decided they needed an escape route, it was good enough for him. He did as Lambert said, climbed on top of the dried well, lowered himself in, and then used the roughness of the stone walls to lower himself.

All he needed now was to slip and break an ankle. It smelled of damp and moss. The stone walls were covered in a slick slime. He used his hip flexors and his thighs to press the outer edge of his feet against the stones.

"Now go," Lambert commanded. "They're coming!"

Hunt said, "Have they broken —" his voice trailed as he shot downwards into the darkness. He didn't have time to yell before he hit the bottom and crumpled to the cold muddy floor.

"*Urgh*," he groaned. He was winded. He looked up and saw Lambert's head peering down from above.

"You okay?"

"*Uh-ha*."

"Move away then, I'm coming down."

Hunt felt around in the darkness. He ran his fingers along the stones and the mud, he was looking for the passageway. He got to his knees and touched the well's walls with his palms.

"Wait ..." he said just as he found the opening.

"Here I come," Lambert shouted.

Hunt dived blindly into the opening. Lambert landed with a thud and groaned and coughed.

"I think I broke a rib," he moaned and held his chest. "We're alive!"

"Over here, there's a tunnel," Hunt said, trying to direct Lambert with his voice. He felt some of the limestone earth come loose and sand and soil fell into his hair. He coughed. It was dusty and dark.

"You have to crawl," Lambert said as he knocked into Hunt's boots.

Arm over arm, he and Lambert crawled through the sodden tunnel. Their heads were down in the narrow passage. They wriggled their bodies and drove with their knees like they would if they were crawling through the mud under low slung barbed wire. Hunt heard noises in the darkness ahead. Rats. He hated rats.

"How far?" Hunt said and got a mouthful of dirt and grit.

"Depends on how crazy the originals were," Lambert said and spat out the soil from Hunt's boots. "There is a stream outside the wire."

CHAPTER EIGHTEEN

Hunt saw a single beam of sunlight in front of him. Dust and particles of dirt floated through it. It made him crawl faster. More purposefully. The end in sight.

When he came to the end of the tunnel, it wasn't open, there were bits of light shining through from outside. He could hear running water. The stream.

"What's going on?" Lambert asked from behind him.

"It's blocked off," Hunt said.

"Push through!"

Lambert was obviously sick of being in the dark and eating the dust in Hunt's wake. Hunt put his hand up against the blockage. It felt cool to the touch, and sharp, like bits of branches and twigs held in place by compacted mud. He gave it a shove. It shook and threw off some debris, but didn't budge.

"Firmer!" Lambert yelled.

"Screw it," Hunt said. He kicked his legs out and drove himself forward. He felt the mud and branches press against his face. He put his hands up and pushed forward. He pressed against it with his forehead and gave a deep throated growl that turned into a silverback-like roar.

"*Argh!*" The compacted twigs and branches came loose and his head broke through into the clear air. Hunt was half in and half out of the tunnel. His eyes adjusted to the light and he saw that they were under a low canopy of semi-coniferous trees. Beams of sunlight streamed through the trees and in the shade it was cool. He pulled himself out of the hole and then reached down and grabbed hold of Lambert's hands. Hunt leaned back and dragged Lambert out. He fell on his arse and Lambert looked up at him with his cut up face and they started to laugh.

"Bloody hell, always the adventure with you, Englishman."

"Come on," Lambert said.

"I'd really like to know where we're going, and what the plan is," Hunt said as he followed Lambert through the forest.

"Ah, but you are in my country now, roast beef. Do as I say. As long as you are my peripheral vision, one eye isn't great for a wide angle."

"Sure," Hunt spun around to make sure they were alone. He heard some distant shouts and engines. They walked along the slightly sloping ground with their backs to the stream. Lambert kept low and felt his way along. When Hunt fell behind he said, "Come on, Normandy, the colonel, has a hunting shack up here. It is deep in the woods."

They turned right from the stream and Hunt could make out the green tiled roof. It was a small, square, dark-varnished and well maintained little cabin. Lambert stepped onto the narrow porch with a length of wood he'd found and smashed a pane of glass. He put his arm through the door, unlocked it, retracted his arm and turned the handle. He pushed it and it swung open. They went inside.

It smelled stale, but felt dry. The colonel kept it in metic-

123

ulously clean condition. There was a single leather chair in front of a wood burning stove. A small galley-style kitchen, and a glass fronted gun cabinet.

Lambert pulled out drawers and opened cupboards and rifled through them. "The colonel's keys are here somewhere," Lambert said. "Make yourself useful, why don't you," he said and glanced back at Hunt. "Make us a cup of coffee."

Hunt furrowed his brow and shook his head, "Bloody surrender monkey, this is no time for coffee!"

Lambert laughed. Just then they heard something outside and they both froze. Lambert tilted his head towards the door. Hunt nodded and took exaggerated strides stepping softly on the wooden floor towards the door. Before he got there, he said in a loud whisper, "Get the guns."

Hunt went to the door, put his back up against the wall, and took a quick look. He couldn't make anything out. Lambert kept looking for the keys. Then, behind the curtain to his right, Hunt saw a nail in the wall with a single copper key attached. He unhooked it, gave a low whistle to get Lambert's attention and lobbed it to him. The Frenchman managed to catch it. Hunt checked outside again. He saw a shimmer. Something, or someone, was moving out there.

LAMBERT WALKED to Hunt's shoulder and handed him a loaded double-barrel shotgun. Hunt took it without taking his eyes off the forest to the front of the cabin. Lambert dangled some keys next to Hunt's head. He glanced at them.

"The colonel's Defender 90," Lambert said close to Hunt's ear. "It's parked out the back next to the woodshed."

"I think there's someone out there," Hunt whispered. "How far is the vehicle?"

"Ten meters."

124

"Can we make it without noise, without drawing attention?"

"No," Lambert answered. They were silent.

"Listen," Lambert said. "I can create a diversion. Distract them. You can get to the four-by-four and get out of here."

Hunt scoffed. It's not that he wasn't grateful. It was just hopeless. "And then, where do I go?"

"You must get to Nice. It's a few hours. Dump that car or swap with another. There is a direct train from Nice to Milan."

"What's in Milan?"

"A man. He is a Frenchman. Also an ex-Legionnaire. He is legendary in the community. He is someone who might help you, but he requires a lot of payment. Everyone only knows him as Louis."

"Milan ..."

"*Oui. Milano.* Along the Piazza del Duomo, there is a flower shop. Tell the old man that you want to buy some garlic ... and you need to speak to Louis Trois."

Lambert put the Defender's key, and the one-sided silver coin in Hunt's hand. Hunt handed him the shotgun.

"Go out the back," Lambert said. "Give him the silver coin."

Hunt heard the loud and unmistakable snap of a dried twig break underfoot.

"We're out of time," Hunt said. He saw the black and navy-blue uniformed armed gendarmes near the stream.

"You must go," Lambert said. "*Bonne chance.*"

———

HUNT CREPT out the back door. He checked his fives-and-twenties and crouched down and ran out across the carpet of dead leaves lying on the cleared land directly behind the lodge. He sprinted into the tree line. He kept low and looked back towards the wooden hunting cabin. His heart was racing. He was hyper-alert. The sounds around him were normal. Forest sounds, running water, bird song. He walked a bit further and found a blue tarp covering a pile of logs stacked ten rows deep. He ducked underneath the tarp and saw an army-green, short-wheelbase Defender hardtop. He unlocked it silently and climbed in and got himself ready.

He prayed that the engine would start first time. As soon as he twisted the ignition, all eyes would be on him. He needed to get out of the killing area as quickly as possible. His only chance was total surprise. He wound down the window to better hear Lambert's deception.

Just then he heard Lambert's voice, loudly proclaiming his presence from the front of the cabin.

"*Hallo! Hallo! Hallo! Philippe Lambert ici! Ne tirez pas! Je ne suis ici que pour chasser des sangliers, mais on dirait que j'ai trouvé un attelage de cochons!*"

Hunt couldn't help but laugh. That was his signal. Lambert told the gendarmes that he was 'hunting boar, but he seemed to have found a team of pigs'. Hunt heard a few shouts in the forest, and the *gendarmes* were aware. Hunt heard a shotgun blast. Immediately he twisted the key in the ignition. The starter motor turned over, but the engine didn't fire. "Come on, come on!" He pressed hard on the accelerator aware that he was in danger of flooding it. He tried again. He twisted hard and pumped the accelerator. It didn't start.

"Oh, god."

He heard something outside the tarpaulin. Lambert shouted from somewhere over to his right hand side, "Go! Go! Go!" Suddenly the tarp lifted and a helmeted and goggled *gendarme* was standing there. Hunt twisted the key. The engine fired. He slammed it into first gear and pressed the accelerator. The Defender lurched forward and sent the rural policeman flying backwards into the logs. Hunt accelerated hard. Rounds thudded into the back and side of the Land

Rover. He ducked instinctively and swerved and then corrected to bring the heavy off-road vehicle back onto the track. That's naughty, he thought. He wasn't sure of the rules of engagement in France, but firing at a fleeing vehicle surely was against them. He bounced up and down and shook from side to side as the 2.2-litre Diesel engine thundered through the forest. He drove aggressively. Tree trunks and branches flashed past him. He had no idea where the track led. He just knew he had to get out of there. He was headed east and he'd keep going that way until he got to somewhere safe.

"WHAT THE HELL IS GOING ON!" Soames' voice boomed. He'd rolled up his sleeves and he was sweating. The screens were a haze of static. "Where the hell is my picture?"

"We've lost the satellite feed," Rishi said and picked up the phone.

"Get it back! *Jesus Christ*. I'm surrounded by amateurs."

Holland looked at Soames nervously and bit the cuticle on his thumb. Soames leaned towards Holland's ear and said, "This is your *fault*. Fix it." He continued, louder, to the room. "Find out where the hell that Land Rover was going." Soames paced.

"And get me the goddamn *gendarmes* commander on the phone!" he bellowed. "I can't believe this ... I can't believe this," Soames said over and over. He picked up his suit jacket off the back of a chair and walked over to the door. Everyone held their breath and watched him go. He turned to face the room and pointed at Holland, "Fix this!"

SOAMES WENT to his office and sharply pulled a drawer open. He roughly bundled a cheap mobile phone out of its box. He fumbled with his thick fingers to pull it open and slip the new SIM card into the small slot. He huffed and puffed and panted as he copied the number down and punched in the digits. London Bridge was lit up in the winter darkness and rain pattered against the glass. He didn't notice the view.

"It's me," Soames said and listened to the voice on the other end. "Yes, I know I said I would never call you, but we have a problem."

He listened again.

"Yes, we have a problem. The thing you want, the thing I need, he has it. I'm sure of it."

He paused again.

"Think, man, think! Why else would he run? He was the last one to see him alive ..." Soames was silent. "Well, I don't know. Either he knows and is making his own play, which would be smart, smarter than I gave him credit for, or, he doesn't know and is running anyway. Either way, we need to get him."

Soames looked behind him quickly to make sure he was alone and listened.

"No! You need it too, don't forget. We made a deal. If you think you can walk away from this thing now, you are very much mistaken."

Soames looked at the rain hitting the window.

"Oh, you think I'm going to owe you, do you? Fine. I'll owe you one. Just make sure you do your job this time ..." Soames hung up the burner and slumped down heavily into his desk chair. He was sweating and wiped his forehead. He reclined and raised his hand to his mouth in the darkness. Then sat forward and pulled the back off the phone, took the battery out, and removed the tiny golden chip from the slot. He put it in his mouth and bit down hard on it until he felt it snap. Had he been overzealous in making the call? No, he didn't think so. It needed to be done.

CHAPTER NINETEEN

MILAN, ITALY

Hunt wore a navy-blue New York Yankees baseball cap and had his collar pulled up. He tried to look casual as he browsed the tourist flyers and leaflets at a kiosk in Milan's central train station. He selected a map from the rack and bought a pack of gum from the Asian gentleman behind the counter. He said, "*Grazie*," and opened the pack and put a soft stick of pink gum in his mouth.

Nothing but an American tourist in town for the Christmas market. The *Piazza del Duomo*, or Cathedral Square, hosted Milan's largest annual Christmas market. It was a ten minute bus ride from the train station. Hunt got himself a small, strong, extra-hot coffee from the station's Starbucks and caught the green M3 bus to the cathedral.

He stepped off the bus and felt the cold winter air on his cheeks. It was still and clear and very crisp.

The crowds were thick. Hunt heard the noise of a rock

band playing, and saw the bright white lights in the square. It was early evening, but the party was in full swing. The *piazza* was filled with people. Hunt took a moment to look up at the Catholic cathedral. It had spotlights shining up at it from the stone and cobbled street below. Its multiple sharp spires gave it a menacing and powerful aura. Below the cathedral, under red canvas, open sided tents and white lights, stall owners sold their wares.

Everything from fruit and vegetables, to works of art, to local *gastronomia* and sweets. There was even one guy selling Union Jack cushions in a range of colours and different shapes and sizes. There was also a giant Christmas tree to the side of the cathedral. It was decorated and lit by blinding white lights. Anything to overcome the dark shroud the black skies cast over the northern Italian city.

Hunt stepped around the outside of the market. He was looking for Louis' flower shop. He walked, from in front of the cathedral, under the arches along the sides of the large square and along the shop frontages. They were mostly tourist traps and official *Duomo* merchandise. Outdoor, gas fired heaters glowed neon-orange as couples in fur coats and leather jackets sipped hot chocolate and mulled wine to the side of the *piazza*. Hunt pulled his baseball cap down lower and stuck his hands deeper in his pockets. He wanted to stop for a strong whisky or a strong coffee, or maybe a strong coffee spiked with a strong whisky, but he kept discipline and kept moving. The mission was paramount.

Opposite the cathedral, behind a row of forlorn looking palm trees, hidden in the corner of the square, Hunt finally found the flower shop. It was called *Fiori Fantastici*. Fantastic Flowers. He saw yellow light from a single desk lamp inside. Otherwise it was dark. The sign on the door said 'closed'.

Hunt pressed down on the brass door handle and pushed. The worn catch gave way and the 'closed' sign bashed on the glass. A brass bell on a string tinkled as he stepped into the warm and floral smelling shop. Sat on a stool, behind a white counter, was a slight, thin, man clipping rose stems with a pair of red-handled pruning shears.

He had bulging, exaggerated, high cheekbones and a large, lumpy, bald head. He looked like his ancestors were Tartars or had a gland disorder.

Hunt saw tattoos on the fingers of his right hand. That, and he was missing the two middle fingers on that hand. He only had an index and pinky. The other two were nubs. Without looking up the man said in Italian, "*Siamo chiusi.*" Hunt didn't respond. The man clipped the rose stem, threw it on the pile on the white countertop and looked up at Hunt. Then he said in English, while gazing at the tall stranger, "We're closed."

He had a heavy French accent. Parisian, Hunt guessed, but could be Bordeaux, for all he knew.

"I'm not here to buy flowers," Hunt said and reached into his trouser pocket. "I need garlic."

The man furrowed his brow. Hunt placed the single sided coin on the counter. The man barely glanced at it as he picked up another rose and clipped the end of it. He pulled some leaves off the steam like he was stripping the skin off a rabbit and said again, "We're closed."

"I thought Italian places stayed open late."

"I don't like tourists."

"You mean you don't like money."

"No, I like money just fine. What I don't like is people touching and not buying." The man, Hunt presumed was Louis, looked up at him. "Why did you ask for garlic?" he asked.

"A mutual friend told me to say it. I thought it was a code for something ..."

"Asking to buy garlic in a flower shop?" Louis scoffed. "Someone is having you on. We don't have any friends in common."

"You're not Louis Trois, then?" Hunt asked. The man didn't respond. Hunt glanced down at his hand, "Because those three fingers on your clipping hand and your accent makes me think you're just the kind of man who could sell me some garlic."

Louis looked up at him blankly again.

"Did they follow you?"

"Who's *they*?"

"Doesn't matter. They. Them. The royal 'we'. The ones in the shadows. The ones always watching. Do you have a phone on you?"

Hunt shook his head, 'no'.

"Good."

"What makes you think I'm being followed?" Hunt asked.

Louis looked him up and down, "Well, aren't you? Why else would you be here ..."

"So, you will help me?"

Louis dropped the corners of his mouth and gave a single shake of his head and went on clipping the rose stem.

"Why not?" Hunt asked.

Louis put his shearing hand in his lap and looked up at Hunt again. He looked for an awkward amount of time.

"When I look at you I don't see someone who can afford my services. I see someone alone. You're alone, aren't you?"

Always have been, Hunt thought.

"You're fumbling around in dark corners looking for a morsel, well, the only thing that gets you friends is gold. You aren't wearing any jewellery. You look too poor to be my friend." He went back to pulling leaves.

"You like jewellery?"

Louis picked up the rose, "Oldest currency in the world," he said.

Hunt stepped forward and Louis glanced at him. Hunt picked up the pen next to the phone and spun a notepad around. He scrawled on the paper and then spun it back so it faced Louis, so he could read it. The florist squinted at the numbers. Hunt stayed where he was. Close to the counter, almost up against it, and he got a better sense how small and slight Louis really was. He looked like a survivor. Hunt looked down at him in an imposing way, and pointed to the numbers scrawled on the notepad.

"Those are —," he started.

"I know what those are," Louis spoke over him. "Is it Switzerland or Luxembourg?"

"Close," Hunt said. "Off-bank safety deposit in Liechtenstein."

Louis clipped the rose stem. He was unmoved. Hunt felt the need to press on. "There's an uncut, ruby red diamond in there," Hunt said.

Louis replaced the flower and took a new one. He pulled off the leaves. "It's about fifty-carats ..."

Louis stopped cutting and looked him in the eye. "Maybe you do have one friend, after all," the Frenchman said. "But, what do I want with a rough diamond?"

"If you help me, it's yours."

Louis kept looking at him. Hunt could see the cogs turning. He could practically feel him salivating at the thought.

"I am expensive," Louis said, "but, I am also fair. What if the cost of the stone is more than the cost of my services?"

Hunt looked up at the ceiling. "If you sell it for more, then, keep what you think is fair. Send me the rest."

"And, if they catch you or you die?"

"Then keep it," Hunt said.

"Well then," Louis said and shook his head. He picked up another long-stemmed rose. "What is my incentive for helping you? I should just kill you now."

"No," Hunt said and shook his head. "I think your business, above all else, is based on trust. If you are untrustworthy once, your customers and potential customers will go somewhere else. The man who gave me that coin," Hunt pointed

133

at the chit in lieu lying silent on the counter top, "Trusted you, so, I trust you. And now, you need to trust me."

There was a pause. Then Louis said, "All right, tell me what you need."

"I need papers," Hunt said. "Real ones, not fake. Never before used. They have to be clean."

"So they are chasing you," Louis said.

"I also need information."

"What kind?"

"The secret kind. I need someone who can get access to most internal systems. Someone good with computers and research. Someone who knows their way around firewalls."

Louis didn't say anything. Hunt held his breath.

"Anything else?" the Frenchman said.

Hunt shook his head. "Not right now."

"Okay," Louis said and stood up. He was barely taller than when he was sitting. He was like a jockey. "You have a place to stay? You have money?"

"No."

"I have a safe house in the city. You can use it. I can have the documents in the next days. The person you are looking for, the one who can crack safes, is in Odessa."

Hunt shook his head slightly. Louis noticed and glanced up at him, "Someone like that, it is better to live outside of the West. And, they don't travel or talk over the airwaves, so you will have to go and meet them."

"I can't travel to Ukraine," Hunt said.

Louis shrugged and dropped the corners of his mouth like a mafioso. "For fifty carats I will get you to Odessa. If the stone is what you say it is ... someone will travel to the bank tonight and verify, if everything is okay, I will arrange what you require."

Hunt nodded. Louis bent and took a big-buttoned calculator from under the counter. He tapped the numbered squares and they *clacked* as he mouthed the sums. The numbers went up and up.

"Six hundred thousand per name," Louis said. "Hundred for the safe house. Flight ... papers ... extra for quick delivery. Twenty-two percent value added tax ..." he hit enter and spun the calculator around. "Shall we say an even two point five million? Dollars," Louis said.

Hunt raised his eyebrows. "Sure," Hunt said and shrugged. "Can you throw in a Glock and a suppressor?"

Louis glanced at the digits on the calculator. Hunt thought he was about to ask for more money.

"Yes," Louis said, "Okay." Then he turned and went into the back of the shop. Hunt waited a few minutes and Louis came back with a folded manila envelope and dropped it with a thud on the counter. "Walking around money," Louis said.

Hunt picked up the envelope and looked inside. He could see at least three different denominations. It must have been close to ten thousand dollars.

The Frenchman reached down and picked the silver single sided coin up between his finger and thumb and dropped it in his right trouser pocket. "I believe your friend will also consider this debt paid," he said.

CHAPTER TWENTY

SOCHI, RUSSIA

Natalia descended the wide, white marble staircase of Mints' mountain compound. Her black, high-heeled leather boots echoed as she stepped down the stairs and she cursed under her breath. She hoped to exit the gaudy palace without being interrupted. It was eerily quiet in the grand entrance hall. White pillars and busts of Roman generals stared blankly from their smooth eyeballs.

She heard "Miss Sukolova!" boom out and echo around the cold marbled entrance and she gasped in surprise. "My apologies, I didn't mean to startle you."

"*Khristos!*" she said with her hand on her chest. "My God, Igor. Do you really need to sneak up on people like that?" she said as she descended.

Igor Agoranov's sunken and dark ringed eyes watched her. He tried to smile, but it looked like a grimace. "The boss," he said and extended an arm from behind his back in the direction of Mints' office.

"What about him?" she asked curtly as she moved to brush past him. She smelled his fish breath as she passed and wanted to gag.

"He has asked to see you ..."

"I have an appointment, it'll have to wait —"

The retired FSB officer grabbed her upper arm and yanked her back hard enough so that she almost lost her balance. At first she was shocked, then furious.

"Let go of me!" she hissed at him and she tried to pull her arm free. Agoranov didn't let go. He pulled her closer to him and took a deep inhale through his nose, smelling her skin. Her face was close to his. She was repulsed. He said, "The boss has asked to see you now."

She pulled away again and gagged and he let go this time. He had a satisfied look on his face. He despised her and despised himself for wanting her, she could tell. She knew. She fixed the waves in her hair and pulled her bright red overcoat back into place.

"Lead on then, *Kretin*," she said.

He stepped back and again swept his arm in a wide arc like he was a waiter welcoming her to her table. She scoffed and walked past him. The liveried footman jumped into action as her boots clattered towards the garishly grand floor-to-ceiling doors.

She had to wait impatiently as he opened them and then the footman had to step into Mints' office to announce her. He saw his boss on the phone and Mints waved her in. The footman stepped aside and Natalia entered. Mints replaced the receiver gently and stood up. He tucked his thumbs under his belt and pulled his trousers up. He stepped away from his desk and removed his thumbs and his trousers immediately sank lower. He came over to air kiss her 'hello' and then gestured to one of the chairs opposite his desk. He held the back of the chair as she sat and pushed it forward for her and said, "Am I inconveniencing you, Natalia?"

It had an air of menace. The hairs on the back of her neck stood up. He stepped away to the mantelpiece and took the lid off a crystal decanter and lifted it to his nose. He sniffed it and, while he poured himself a drink, she said, "No, not at all."

He picked up the glass of vodka and said, "Good. Even though it's a lie. Good ..."

He sat heavily in his chair and sipped it and smacked his lips. He didn't offer her one. The manners of a peasant. You can take them from the fields ... he glanced at her and she perked up and smiled sweetly at him.

"Don't *damn well* look at me like that," he said quietly and leaned forward slightly and placed his glass down. "I'm not one of your helpless assets," he said and leaned back and studied her with his head pressed back on the high-backed chair.

"Oh, no?" she said sweetly. She couldn't help goading when she was around him. It was like a defence mechanism against her helplessness.

He lifted and shook his head, "No. You are my asset. I own you."

"Do you?" she said and held her plastered, perfect ballerina's smile.

"I do," he said and looked up at the portrait of Stalin above the mantelpiece. "But, I've been thinking. Maybe you need some incentive."

He looked back at her and raised his eyebrows. He rubbed his pockmarked, bullfrogs neck and she swallowed when he glanced away. She was holding her posture and her breath like a yoga pose.

"Then, I was thinking. The whip or the caviar? And I said to myself, 'why not both'."

Mints' eyes were half-closed. He looked out at her from

under those heavy eyelids. This was his dangerous look, like a viper that puffs itself up to look bigger. When Anatoly Mints looked like he might fall asleep, people should beware. She'd seen it before. It was like a read at the card table. She knew he was holding a pair of aces.

"You know I'll kill her, don't you," he said. "If you ever betray me ..." It was said quietly, but with force. A threat, the gravity of which, was self-sustaining. She nodded imperceptibly. She knew he would. "Wipe that sick goddamn smile off your face," he said, and she did.

"Now, the caviar," he said. "How would you like to be free?"

She swallowed again. She breathed deeply. She was elated, but tried not to let it show. Her mind skipped to the bargain, what was it he wanted?

He nodded. "Good then, do this thing for me, and I will let you go ..." he picked up his glass and gulped the vodka down. For all his expensive tastes he still liked the stuff distilled in the countryside by farmers and peasants in their stills at home. "My little birds tell me that the general's bodyguard, the one you left alive when you should have killed him, is just across the Black Sea."

She feigned surprise, because that's what she thought he would want to see. Surprise that he was able to acquire this information. That he had the knowledge and influence to find out what whole intelligence agencies couldn't. Money, and the kind of money that Mints' had, created a queue of people waiting to share information with him. If he liked it, he made them very wealthy.

"Go and find out what he is doing there ... bring him to me with whatever he has on him. Or, bring him to me dead with whatever he has on him. That bastard has been a fox in my henhouse for the last time."

There you go, she thought, you can't pull the fields out of the peasant.

"And if I bring him to you —"

"You can go. Go to Paris, or Milan, or Moscow and buy nice clothes and shop at the Gucci store."

If that was what he thought her ambitions were, she'd done a better job concealing her true self from him than she'd imagined.

"And what about her?"

"She stays. That is the bargain," he said. He was smug. He was congratulating himself for reading the situation so well.

"It's a devil's bargain," she said quietly and immediately regretted it and looked away. When she glanced back at him, he was smiling.

He cocked his head with a perverted grin and said, "Well then, I must be the devil, because that is my bargain. You can win your freedom, but she stays. She wouldn't leave me anyway ..."

"You don't think?"

He shook his head and pursed his fat, cracked lips. "No," he said. "After all these years, she cannot leave. Where would she go?"

Natalia let him have the victory. He'd already given away more than he knew.

"Is that it?" she asked curtly and stood in one graceful movement. Her back was still straight, her neck long, and her hands clasped to her front. As she turned to go, out of the corner of her eye, she saw, first, his mouth drop in sudden disbelief. His face said 'the insolence, how dare she leave before being dismissed' and then pure, violent, rage. His eyes were wide and his mouth curled in a snarl. He stood up and as he was about to rush from behind the desk and attack her, she turned and he stopped abruptly, suddenly conscious of himself.

"Yes, okay," she said. "I will do it. In return for my freedom."

A smile like an oil slick spread across his lips. The

footman pulled the doors open and she left. She heard him shout after her, "As if you had a choice! As if I even gave you a choice!"

She smiled to herself as the yells faded and the doors shut. When she was sure she was alone her smile dropped and she fell forward. She caught herself against one of the Roman busts and her eyes filled with tears. As she looked into the clear, dead eyes of Caesar, she knew what she had to do.

CHAPTER TWENTY-ONE

ODESSA, UKRAINE

Hunt sat opposite a Ukrainian man onboard a Bombardier Global Express private charter jet. Louis had introduced him to Hunt as 'the most wanted man in Kiev.' It hadn't filled Hunt with confidence.

Kyrilo, the Ukrainian, was wearing a black suit that was two sizes too big for him. He was the size and shape of a powerlifter, all trapezius muscles and no neck. He wore these dainty round wire spectacles that bent outward to fit around his bulging temples. And, he didn't speak. He hadn't said a word for the entire three hour flight, he just sat there, facing backwards, looking out the window on the hop from Milan to Odessa.

Louis had come through. Hunt had, in his breast pocket, a diplomatic passport in the name of Hector Reyes from Liberia. The small West African country was the world's biggest exporter of blood diamonds, which poured across the

142

border from Sierra Leone. Was it Louis' idea of a joke, Hunt wondered, considering the payment method? He didn't know the French, or Legionnaire, sense of humour. It wouldn't have surprised him. He had the requested Glock in a shoulder holster, and a small duffel bag with a brand new laptop, and the suppressor for the weapon. He kept General Patrick's watch in his inside breast pocket. He travelled light.

The thing about the passport was, it was only useful once. The days of multiple fake passports were over. Now that technology was on par with the high quality fakes, and information sharing between countries and businesses was commonplace. Spies and people trying to move under the radar would always be linked to the biometric data on a passport. It was a burner passport situation now. Use it once and then destroy the identity. It was the joker in the pack, and Hunt had to play it strategically. So, the plan to get him into Ukraine was an altogether different approach.

As technology had improved and getting access to a country's databases had become more difficult, the Americans had begun recruiting more and more agents in foreign controlled border agencies. Either to change the uploaded biometric data, like iris scans, finger prints, and facial recognition associated with a particular fake passport, or to assist them on the ground in a more analogue way. Kyrilo was one of those foreign agents. A Ukrainian Central Intelligence Agency asset. Hard as a hammer and as bent as a sickle.

As they approached Odessa airport, Kyrilo pulled out a black bag from under his seat, unzipped it, and held up a black hood and handcuffs.

"What, no orange jumpsuit?" Hunt asked.

"Ukraine is getting more savvy with public relations," the massive Ukrainian said without a hint of irony or a smile. Hunt was impressed with his calm and measured tone.

"So, I guess you don't do that anymore ..." Hunt said.

Kyrilo didn't respond. He didn't ask Hunt's permission

either. Kyrilo clasped the handcuffs over Hunt's wrists and whipped the hood over his head.

"Can't we wait until we land?" Hunt asked.

"You are prisoner now. Resist temptation to speak."

Hunt shut his mouth and sat quietly under the hood. It was difficult to breathe and the hot air from his mouth made his head feel warm and claustrophobic. What Hunt knew was that the Ukrainians had an agreement with the Americans. The Central Intelligence Agency would never have to reveal a prisoner's identity during a rendition. Kyrilo held authentic CIA paperwork for the prisoner rendition, for the possibility that the Ukrainian State Border Guard Service requested it. Both he and Hunt doubted they would.

The aircraft landed and taxied a long way. Kyrilo lifted Hunt up by the armpit and guided him to the exit. Hunt heard the private jet's main door open and immediately felt the icy-blast of Black Sea air. It was snowing and the wind whipped around the cabin. Hunt couldn't see anything, but he could feel and hear it. The Ukrainian guided him down the stairs.

"There are two border guards," Kyrilo said to Hunt. He greeted them in Ukrainian and pulled Hunt along. Hunt heard the shuffle of papers, but they didn't stop walking.

"Stop here."

Hunt stopped. He stood in the cold wind and snow. His hands were exposed at the front of his body and freezing. Then he heard the men saying their goodbyes and the sound of a heavy car door opened. Kyrilo put his breeze block of a hand on Hunt's neck and pushed his head down to help him duck into the car. He heard the satisfying thump as the door closed and shut out the noise of the snowstorm from outside.

Hunt tried to rub his hands together. Then the other door opened and the whole vehicle rolled from side to side as the massive Ukrainian got in. Hunt felt Kyrilo's hand on his head again and the hood came off.

"Welcome to my country," Kyrilo said as he leaned over and unlocked the handcuffs. "I hope you will have a pleasant stay."

"I'm sure I will, big lad. I'm sure I will."

The driver of the luxury sedan glanced at Hunt in the rearview mirror as he pulled off and drove out of the airport. They were five miles from the centre of the city. Hunt looked out the window at the falling snow as it whipped around the sedan. It was a whiteout. Kyrilo went back to staring silently outside and didn't speak again for the rest of the journey.

THE DRIVER DROPPED Hunt in front of the Odessa Fine Arts Museum. It backed onto the waterfront and was a short walk from the centre of the city.

"Thanks, Kyrilo. If I ever need someone to talk to, I'll give you a call …"

Kyrilo nodded as Hunt went to close the car door. Just before he closed it, the big Ukrainian leaned over and said, "You need anything you contact Louis."

Hunt got the message. Kyrilo's job was done. He shut the door and looked up at the tall marble columns of the museum. Greek culture and design, via the Romans, really had invaded the world.

They way the cold bit into his skin and penetrated through his clothes reminded him of training in the Norwegian Arctic.

Hunt had been given very specific instructions. He'd been told to go to a coffee shop. It was a fifteen minute walk along the waterfront. It was bitterly cold. He jogged in bursts to keep warm. The air tore at his throat and burned his lungs. He kept going until he saw the Potemkin Stairs start to rise up like a mountain to his left. They were an impressive sight, but Hunt didn't have time for sightseeing.

He turned right and headed into the centre of Odessa. There were quaint tree-lined avenues leading into the centre of the city. It was cold, snow lay on the ground, and there was very little traffic, but to Hunt, the shape of the buildings and architecture reminded him of Paris.

If he wasn't on the run for his life, Odessa seemed like a place he would enjoy taking a stroll around under the street-lights at midnight. His eyelashes had bits of white flecks of snow in them. He blinked and read the street signs. The thought of a toasty-warm indoors and hot, fresh coffee sounded very appealing. Then, off a square, he saw a small side street. The snow crunched under his feet as he walked past a frozen fountain. None of the shops or boutiques seemed to have names outside them, so he went to the one that looked most like a coffee shop. It had stacks of chairs chained to tables all covered in white snow. He stepped in and behind the counter in big, capital orange letters he saw the name AFRIKA. Odd name for a coffee shop in the middle of Odessa, but there it was, just as he'd been instructed.

The interior followed the theme. The ceiling had large, upturned, woven reed baskets hanging from it, like lamp-shades. It was all woven-reed chairs and Africa-patterned orange cushions. The lights were on, but it was empty. There was only one server behind the counter. She greeted him in Ukrainian and gestured to the empty coffee shop.

Hunt stamped his boots on the mat at the entrance and breathed in the warm air. He took off his coat and went to sit at a table in the back corner with a view of the entrance. He didn't know exactly what he was doing there, only that he had been told to go there and wait. That was exactly what he now did. He ordered a large, frothy, very hot cappuccino and waited.

THE WAITRESS CAME and took his cup away after he'd finished. He ordered a large Americano with hot milk. He wasn't usually one for sweet drinks, but he poured in two sachets of brown sugar and took a delicate sip. It was far too hot. He set it down and waited some more.

He checked his watch. Almost thirty minutes. His second coffee was nearly finished when the glass front door opened with a bang and the sudden shock of cold air blew in. Hunt and the waitress both looked up at the same time. A big guy in a black motorcycle outfit and black, full-face helmet stood in the open doorway and stamped his boots. He walked into the coffeeshop and unzipped his jacket. Without taking his helmet off he said, "Hector Reyes?"

Hunt nodded and the man pulled out a yellow reinforced envelope and handed it to him. Hunt looked at the envelope and reached out to take it. The motorcycle rider let go before he'd taken hold of it properly and it slipped. He caught it and was surprised by the weight. The guy in the black gear turned and his boots squeaked on the wooden floor as he walked out. There was a fresh blast of cold air before the door slammed shut.

The waitress was looking at Hunt. He raised his eyebrows and looked back at the envelope in his hands. After a few seconds she went back to cleaning behind the counter. Hunt pulled the envelope open and took out a computer tablet with headphones attached. It had a sticky note on the front that said, 'you turn me on'. He gave a silent chuckle.

He stuck the headphones in his ears and turned the tablet on. The backlit screen came on and then the tablet started to vibrate. He was receiving a video call. He answered. The image on the screen was dark, but he could see shadows. Not enough to make out who was on the other end of the video though.

"Hello?" Hunt said.

"I didn't think you'd make it," the voice said. The sound

that came through was distorted, like someone was speaking through a voice changer. It was mechanical, like the person on the other end had had a tracheotomy.

"Who are you?" Hunt asked.

"Are you Hector Reyes?" the voice replied.

Hunt nodded, "You know I am."

"I need to be sure. I need you to state your name and the date."

"I'm not comfortable doing that ..."

"Well, then, this conversation is over. Goodbye."

"Wait," Hunt said and took a deep breath to buy him a few seconds. "Okay. Hector Reyes, twenty-ninth of December."

"Do you have any recording devices?"

"No," Hunt said.

"Good. Now, how may I help you?"

Hunt glanced around the coffee shop and over his shoulder. Still empty. "Don't worry, she doesn't speak English," the voice said, referring to the waitress.

"How do I know you're not law enforcement?" Hunt asked.

"You don't. You'll just have to trust me, won't you?"

"How can I do that," Hunt said rhetorically, thinking out loud, more than anything.

"Do you trust Louis?"

Hunt looked at the dark outline on the screen and said nothing.

"I wouldn't either," the voice said. "Maybe you'd be smart to walk away. After all, you could get in a lot of trouble. I know, and I am telling you that you could get in trouble."

Hunt shook his head unconsciously. He was already in a lot of trouble. At the moment, he had no idea how deep, or how far, the mire of excrement extended.

"No," he said. "I need to find out what is happening. Trouble or no trouble."

"All right. Then, how can I help you?"

"I'm trying to find out some information," Hunt said. "The classified kind. The kind that gets you charged under the Official Secrets Act. Can you help me?"

"Tell me what you need."

"Less than a week ago, a senior British Army officer was killed in central London. It's been covered up and I am being put in a frame. I need to know what information there is, and what there is implicating me in it. Why're they after me, what is it that General Patrick Sanders was up to that got him killed."

The voice was silent. Hunt sat looking at the still, dark screen. Then, thinking he'd lost the connection, or it'd frozen, he said, "Hello?"

"I'm thinking," the voice said. "Did you bring the laptop with you like you were instructed?"

Hunt nodded.

"Has it been turned on or used in any way?"

Hunt shook his head.

"Good. Give me twenty-four hours. I will use the laptop to contact you. Don't turn it on until then. When you leave here, destroy this tablet, especially the serial number. Never use it again."

The screen went completely black.

CHAPTER TWENTY-TWO

THE CLUBHOUSE, LONDON

Soames walked into the operations room and leaned in the door. He caught Rishi's eye and asked, "Where's Holland?"

Rishi pointed down the corridor and said, "He moved his office down here. I think he was on a call ..."

Soames tapped the frame of the door in thanks and went to find him. He saw Holland behind some frosted glass and tapped on the door and opened it. Holland was on the phone. He held up one finger and Soames stood there holding the door open and waited.

"And you're sure?" Holland said. "Okay. No, thank you. Thanks for letting me know."

He was quiet.

"Yes, no, I will sort it out. Thank you. Goodbye."

Holland hung the phone up and put his face in his hands and exhaled.

"What was that?" Soames asked.

Holland puffed his cheeks out and exhaled. "You're not not going to believe this Gerry, sir, I mean, maybe you will, you probably will ..."

"Spit it out, Tom."

"That was GCHQ."

Soames was suddenly interested. He stepped inside the bare office and shut the door. "What did they want?"

"After you told me about the mole, I called GCHQ and asked for a trace on all mobile phone calls emanating from this office. I mean, they are monitored anyway, but I put a request in for a trace."

Soames felt the blood run from his face and an emptiness in the base of his stomach. "And?" he said quietly. He already knew the answer.

"They traced a call. Unknown number. Unknown phone. Classic burner behaviour."

"From this building?" Soames asked.

Holland nodded.

"Which office?"

"They can't tell that, but they knew the number it dialled. It was scrambled by some sort of encryption, but it was a call to Russia."

"Oh my God," Soames said and turned away from Holland and paced the room. "I mean, good thinking, first of all, to request the trace. That was smart ..." Soames said, thinking out loud. "Pity about the scrambler. And, they have no more information than that?" he asked and turned back to Holland.

Holland shook his head, "No, but - bloody hell - we now know for a certainty that someone in this building is leaking information. We found the source of the leak ..."

"Sure, but we don't know who it was, right? Or, if that was even a call about something to do with what we're doing here ..." Soames clenched his jaw. He was not being calm. He could give the game away right here. Holland was quiet and looked at Soames.

"We need to be sure ..." Soames started to say, more to fill the silence than anything, but he stopped himself and waited for Holland to react.

"Yeah, no, ah, you're right, sir. We can't know for certain. Should I ask them to keep the trace going, or call it off?"

Soames wanted to smile at the boy. He had minerals. Calling Soames' bluff. Checking his behaviour. "Keep it going," Soames said. "Let's see if we can catch the bastard."

"Yes, sir."

"Good work, Tom. Very good work," Soames said as he walked to the door. He pulled it open and Holland asked him, "What was it you wanted to see me about?"

Soames looked at him, "Sorry?"

"Just now, you came down to look for me about something, what was it?"

"Oh, ah, no, nothing. This is more important, that can wait." Soames stepped out of the office and then stopped, he turned to look at Holland.

"Sir?" Holland said.

"Actually, the reason I came down ... it's a bit silly really, but you know, with all of this that's been going on, and especially now around the holidays. I wanted to invite you out for a drink ... you know, chinwag. Blow off some steam. I'm sure you're busy though, so never mind ..."

"No, that sounds great," Holland said unexpectedly. "It'll give us a chance to speak more about the case."

"Great," Soames said. "I'll have the work-wife call down with the details."

"Should I invite any of the others?" Holland asked.

Soames smiled. "Let's keep things between us for now," Soames said. "Wouldn't want to make them jealous. One on one time with the boss and all ..."

"Understood," Holland said and nodded.

"Okay," Soames said. "I'll see you later."

Holland just sat there smiling at him with dead eyes.

Soames left the office and clenched his fists and his jaw as he walked down the corridor. He thought a vein in his head might explode. His heart was racing. This was a disaster. On his way back to his office he walked past Madeline, his secretary, whom he called his 'work wife'.

"Get me a list of all outside numbers to Tom Holland's phone in the last hour, will you, Madeline?"

"Certainly, Mister Soames," she said and picked up the phone to request the details.

SOAMES STUDIED THE PRINTOUT. It was a list of numbers dialled from Holland's office phone. He used a gold ball-point pen, a gift from the Foreign Secretary after the successful raid on the *MV Nisha* some years before. He underlined the numbers and put little stars next to the relevant ones. He looked down at the pen. He felt the weight of it in his hand. He felt the importance of it. Spy masters and field operatives never got recognition. Successes were unknown, while failures were infamous. He'd worked in the shadows his whole career. Hunt had been integral to his getting on in his job. He'd been languishing. Then, Holland, young and green had stumbled into intelligence about a terror plot against central London. Hunt was the architect of the mission to raid and subdue the suspected vessel in the English Channel. A potentially catastrophic event neutralised. Soames' career had flourished since. Now, all of that was at risk. His career. His reputation. The nice little nest egg he was gradually accumulating. He picked up the phone and used the back of the pen to dial the number for GCHQ.

"Stevens," the GCHQ analyst answered. He sounded overworked and under-sexed. Soames breathed deeply through his mouth.

"I'm calling about the trace one of mine has ordered," Soames said.

"Mister Holland, yes, sir," Stevens said. He sounded nervous. It was unusual to receive a call from an Intelligence Director. Soames felt he must know he'd done something wrong.

"We're still following up on the number, sir, the destination number, there is a sophisticated encryption —"

"No," Soames said abruptly. He realised his mistake and lowered his voice and slowed his words. "It was a mistake, Stevens, was it?"

"Yes, sir."

"It was an internal error," Soames said.

"But, the burner, sir, the pattern, it's very unusual."

"I said forget about it," Soames said. "Cancel the trace, it's part of a classified mission, above your pay grade, understand?"

"Yes, sir. The phone has since gone dead anyway, sir. Cardinal rule of burner phones, single use only."

"Good. Good," Soames said. "Stevens. I'll remember the name for my report."

Silence.

"You've done a good job here," Soames said.

"Yes, sir," the analyst said. "I'm already three hours past the end of my shift anyway, so only too happy if you've sorted it internally, sir."

"Good man," Soames said and hung up. He lifted the pen to the corner of his mouth and twisted it and sucked on the end. It had small indentations all around the base from his chewing and oral fixation with it. He leaned forward and dialled Holland's office phone. He answered on the first ring.

"On second thoughts, Tom, let's meet in Notting Hill," Soames said.

"Notting Hill?"

"Some new intelligence has just come across my desk,

Tom. Something they found at Hunt's flat. I want to check it out and then we can go for that drink."

"I thought the forensics teams had cleared the flat ..."

"It's something significant," Soames said and checked his watch, "I have to brief the Chief. I'll meet you over there, say ninety-minutes?"

"Yes, sir," Holland said.

"It's top secret, Tom. Don't mention this to anyone ..."

SOAMES ARRIVED IN THE DARKNESS. It was a cold and miserable evening. Only a few people were brave enough to be on the streets. He paid the black cab driver in cash and didn't speak too much. He got him to drop him a few blocks away. The rectangular concrete block of flats was right at the top of Notting Hill. It looked like a typical local council block built in the sixties. People who didn't know what it was would have assumed it was social housing. Soames pulled his collar up and his dark fedora down. He glanced over his shoulder before he entered the walkway made of concrete slabs and walked up the grey stairwell lit by flickering fluorescent lights. The waterproof over-trousers he wore made rhythmic hiss, hiss, hiss sounds as he climbed and his trouser legs rubbed against each other. His rubber shoe covers meant his footsteps were quiet. He didn't see anyone and no-one saw him.

There was police tape across the entrance of the flat's door. Soames unlocked it and pushed it open. The flat was dark and quiet. The only light came from the haloed street lights. He ducked under the police tape and entered. His breathing was shallow. The exertion of climbing those stairs and the eeriness of the cold, empty flat played with his mind. Soames took out a heavy duty, black, metal flashlight. He flicked the beam on and shone it around the room and said,

"Jesus Christ, Hunt." He pushed the front door until it was only just ajar and left it like that.

He felt the cold coming in. The place was bare. A single wooden chair sat next to the plastic outdoor dining table. How could anybody live like this? Soames heard something in the kitchen and he jumped. He fumbled with the flashlight and spun and focussed the beam on the kitchenette. As he did he heard a meow. "Bloody hell," he said and caught his breath. He put his black, leather gloved hand on his chest and felt his heart beating.

"Damn cat."

Flea, Hunt's black and white stray, sat on the counter and watched Soames. He gave another hungry meow. Soames turned off the flashlight and sat in the chair to the right of the door. "Never mind, cat," Soames said in the darkness, "He'll be here soon."

SOAMES WANTED to check his watch. He was sure Holland was late, but the faff of taking off his gloves and turning on the torch to check, dissuaded him. "We'll give it another ten, before we start looking for him," Soames said quietly to the cat. Then he heard the bottom entrance door slam below and footsteps coming up the cold concrete steps. After a few moments Soames saw a shadow in the gap between the frame and the door. He was breathing through his nose as he waited. His head felt light headed. His heart was thumping in his chest. He hoped he could still do it after all these years.

"Gerry?" he heard Holland's voice and then the door creaked as he pushed it open. Holland stepped in under the barrier tape and Soames heard his hand brushing the surface of the wall looking for the light switch. Soames' eyes were already adjusted to the dark. He stood up. Holland flicked the switch, but nothing happened. Just the cat meowed and

Holland jumped and cried out. Then he realised it was a cat and said, "Goddamn it. Hello kitty," he put his hand out to stroke it, but Flea hissed and jumped off the kitchen counter. Holland felt in his pockets for his phone to use for some light. He must have heard Soames move.

"Hello?" Holland said.

Soames flicked the flashlight on and shone the powerful beam right in Holland's face.

"They cut the power to the flat," Soames said.

"Gerry, Jesus Christ, you scared me," Holland said. "I didn't see you there. Wait, were you hiding?" he asked as he covered his eyes from the light. "Were you hiding just now?"

"Come in the kitchen here," Soames said and pointed with his gloved hand. Holland turned to look in the adjoining kitchenette, and, as he did, Soames ran up behind him and used the heavy metal flashlight as a truncheon. He brought the weight of the torch down on the back of Holland's head. Soames heard the crunch as the sharp metal caught the hair and skin on the back of Holland's skull. The tall Secret Intelligence Service Officer fell forward. His body crumpled and his head hit the cold linoleum kitchen floor. Soames followed up by climbing on Holland's back and swinging wildly down on his defenceless colleague.

Holland reached back and tried to cover the side of his face and back of his head but Soames brought the heavy steel bar down on his back and head again and again and again. Soames heard the crunch as bones in Holland's hands and wrists broke under the force of the club. Holland let out a silent moan. Spit and saliva dribbled from the corner of his mouth.

Breathing heavily, Soames got uneasily to his feet and flicked the flashlight on. What he saw sickened him. Holland lay with his arse in the air, the weight of his body resting on his head, which was turned to the side. Blood was streaked across the linoleum floor. Soames sucked in deep breaths. He just breathed and tried to recover and looked down at what he'd done. When he'd gathered himself, he knelt behind Holland's head and used one hand to turn it skyward, so he was looking at his eyes. With the other he bashed down on his contorted face. Whack, whack, whack. The sound was the thump and crack of metal on teeth and bone.

Soames was bashing Holland's face in to make his corpse harder to identify. The blood pooled around his head. When he was sure Holland wasn't breathing, and enough fragments of tooth, lip and gum were lying all over the kitchen floor, Soames went through Holland's pockets and removed everything. He put them into a black plastic bag he'd brought with him. He turned the flashlight to the scene once more, just to double check.

The beam caught the bright reflection of the cat's eyes. Soames sighed. He stepped over the body and opened the fridge. There was an open tin of cat food. He tipped the contents onto the floor next to Holland's bashed-in face. It landed with a congealed slap on the floor.

"Now you've got some company," Soames said. He was still out of breath. The cat meowed again. Soames placed the flashlight on the counter top and reached into his jacket. He pulled out a glass, a small whisky tumbler, that was in a clear plastic bag. He opened the zip-lock and pulled the glass out in his gloved hand. It still smelled faintly of the scotch Hunt had been drinking on Christmas Day. Soames used a large piece of clear sellotape to lift a smudge of a fingerprint off the glass. He placed the sellotape on the glass in front of the bulb of the flashlight and then gently peeled it off. He flicked off the flashlight, dropped it on the body, and wiped the tumbler down. He stuffed it into the black bag along with the other items.

Before he left the flat, Soames pulled off his over-trousers, shoe covers, and then his gloves, and put them all into the black bag. He folded the top of the black bin bag and rolled it up neatly and put it under his arm. Now, he was just some old man out for a walk.

He ducked under the police tape, pulled the door shut and locked it, and hurried down the stairs. With any luck, it would be weeks before they discovered Holland's body and more before they identified him. Out of the entrance to the building Soames turned left and walked down the steep drop of Portobello Road. The streets were empty as he headed for Ladbroke Grove and Kensal Green Cemetery. He felt the cold whip of wind as he crossed the bridge into Kensal Town. He ripped a small hole in the bag so it would fill with water, re-tied the top of it so it was secure and, without stopping, he threw it from the middle of the bridge into the river below. In a few hours it would be pulled down by the current, flow past the City of London, into the Thames, and out into the English Channel.

He schemed as he walked, head down, hands deep in his pockets, to the nearest tube station. What would the working theory be? Hunt and Holland colluded to steal the intelligence. Holland had called Hunt from a burner phone inside MI-6. Holland went to meet him at the only place they could meet and Hunt killed him. That was now two murders that Hunt had committed. After all, who were they going to believe.

CHAPTER TWENTY-THREE

Soames went home. Reverend was barking when he got there.

"*Shush*, Reverend."

The white terrier obeyed him and sat down. Soames went to the kitchen to feed his dog and as he was putting pellets into his bowl his mobile phone buzzed. The pellets pinged off the stainless steel bowl and Reverend tucked in. Soames went to the hallway to check his phone. It was from Rishi. It said: 'No idea where Tom is, boss. I think I have something'.

Soames was on his way back to the Clubhouse anyway. He'd speak to Rishi when he got there. After all, Rishi was heading up the hunt for his rogue operative now. Soames could hear Reverend's name tag clinking against the metal bowl as he gobbled his supper. Soames picked up his keys and wallet and left.

THIRTY MINUTES later he walked into the operations room. It was only Rishi and two other analysts sitting under the harsh brightness of the fluorescent lighting in the basement.

"What've you got?" Soames said.

"All right, sir? Do you know where Mister Holland is?" Rishi asked.

Soames shook his head, "No, but I'm here, so tell me what's going on."

"We put out a grey notice, sir, Tom thought it would be good to have the other intelligence agencies aware, without alerting law enforcement, as you wanted to keep it low profile."

"Spit it out," Soames said through clenched teeth. He specifically had not wanted Interpol or any other agencies involved. He suddenly felt much better about the lanky intelligence officer lying on Hunt's cold kitchen floor with rigor mortis setting in. Soames inadvertently checked the clock. Yes, rigor was definitely setting in by now.

"We've had a hit sir, someone with access commented under the notice."

"Who?"

"A member of the public calling themselves Wooley Stone."

Soames' bushy eyebrows danced as his interest piqued, "What did it say?"

"I'll show you," Rishi said and went to his terminal. Soames followed and Rishi turned the monitor so Soames could see. Under a grainy picture of Hunt, Soames read the comment out loud, "I saw this man in Italy on the twenty-seventh. You want to know where: ThrillFX and bring the *nal*." Soames stood upright and looked at Rishi. "What the hell does that mean?"

"It's Dark Web slang," Rishi said. "It's their username and money. They'll tell us where he is if we pay them."

"Well, have you done it yet?" Soames asked impatiently.

"I was waiting for authorisation from Mister Holland."

"I'm giving it to you. We might have caught a break here," Soames said begrudgingly. Maybe Holland wasn't as much of a moron as he'd thought. Too smart for his own good, evidently. Soames wondered what other little surprises were waiting for him behind doors two and three. "Where did this joker send the message from?"

"I traced the IP address from Iran and about twelve other countries. No way to tell ..." Rishi said.

"Our window of opportunity is closing here, find out how much he wants," Soames said.

"Already done, sir," Rishi said.

"Well?"

"Six hundred thousand dollars," Rishi raised his eyebrows and prepared to flinch at Soames' response.

"Do it," Soames said calmly. "Take it out of the operational budget. I'll explain it to the Foreign Secretary."

Rishi nodded. He looked relieved. Soames turned to walk out of the room, before he got to the door he turned around and said, "Oh, and, ah, congratulations, Rishi."

"On what, sir?"

"Your promotion to Team Director. Until Holland turns up, I need someone in charge, now, that's you. And, that goes for the rest of you too," Soames said addressing the other analysts in the room. "Work hard and you'll rise fast." He looked back at Rishi. "I'll look for Holland, you look for Hunt, understand?" Rishi stood there nodding, taking in the news. "Good work," Soames said and left the room.

BACK ON THE way into his office, Soames said without stopping, "Get me Simon Mansfield."

Only then he realised it was the middle of the night and his secretary wasn't there. He sat down heavily at his desk and picked up his phone. He checked his little black notebook and punched in the number. Foreign ringtone. The line connected and Soames heard background noise. Men shouting and the wash of water.

"This better be bloody good," Mansfield shouted down the line, "I'm interrupting my big game fishing trip for this!"

Mansfield was a large, loud, brash, and pompous ex-special forces officer who had been thriving off his political connections and military résumé for decades.

"Shut up and listen," Soames said. He'd used Mansfield's expertise enough in the past. When foreign intelligence agencies want to do business with people their governments can't, or when it was better for some unofficial third party to be used for a particular mission, Mansfield was the man to speak to.

Mansfield just laughed. He was the kind of man who loudly blurted out things at dinner parties that others were too shy, or too subtle, to mention. Then he'd just throw his head back and slap you on the back and down his drink.

"Hold on Gerry," Mansfield said. Soames heard him shout to someone else, "That's it Bob, you got him! You got him!"

Soames waited. Mansfield came back. "Sorry, Gerry, Bob just hooked a massive marlin. What can I do you for?"

"Do you have any good boys at the moment? Men who can do a clean up job without making too much of a mess?"

"Where?" Mansfield asked.

"Europe."

The line was quiet.

"Christ. Europe, Gerry, you sure? That's your backyard ..."

"Yes," Soames said impatiently and leaned forward as he massaged his forehead. "But they need to be clean and slick and not make a noise."

"Yeah, I know some guys, but they work as a team, Gerry. Two of them. Ex-Delta. They're American, which means they're expensive and my usual fee on top."

"I don't care what it costs," Soames said. "Get off that goddamn fishing boat and get them stood-up and operational."

"What's the detail, Gerry, what do I tell them?"

"I'll have more for you soon, just get the pieces moving around the board. The target is one of ours ... gone rogue. He's been burned. He has stolen data that we need back and your guys need to put him in the dirt, understand?"

The line was quiet.

"Sounds serious," Mansfield said.

"Tell them not to mess around with this guy, Simon," Soames said. "He's ruthless and he won't stop."

"Sounds a bit like you, Gerry."

Soames ignored him.

"You worried he is going to come after you next?" Mansfield asked.

"Listen, get off the boat. Get the guys stood up. Wait for my instructions. Location to follow."

"Right, I —" Mansfield started.

Soames put the phone down.

CHAPTER TWENTY-FOUR

Hunt walked down the snow-covered, tree-lined pavement in the Moldavanka area of the city, near the centre of the Odessa old town. He checked the crumpled piece of paper he'd written the directions down on and then looked up and checked the street names. It was early evening and light was fading.

He only knew his contact's username, *Pyro_glitch*. He didn't know if it was a he or a she. He'd been given an address and told to go down into the Odessa catacombs. Hunt hadn't even known that catacombs existed in Odessa.

They'd found bodies and bones down there, but mostly from the NKVD, Soviet secret police, assassinating people during the Second World War. The tunnels under the city were over twelve-hundred miles long and there were purported to be over a thousand separate entrances. They contained caves, crevasses, and underground lakes. If you wanted to get lost, or not to be seen, the catacombs were as good a place as any in the world. He hoped finding his way out of the black, cold maze would be easier than finding directions to the entrance he'd been given.

He turned left and walked past a Soviet-style block of

flats. All concrete and square blocks. Around the back he found a row of garages. He checked the numbers. The door to the one he wanted was down. He flicked his head torch on and checked the quiet darkness around him. It was empty. He pulled the garage door up and it clanked and rattled and squealed as it came to rest.

He went in. A rat scurried along the wall. At the back of the garage was an old black tarpaulin covered in a fine film of dust. He pulled on a corner and lifted it up. There was a hole in the concrete floor of the garage. He moved closer and shone the white light into the hole. He saw stairs leading into the depth below.

"Stuff this," he said out loud. He looked out into the night in two minds. His breathing was shallow and he felt his pulse popping in his neck. He walked back to the garage door and pulled it shut. It closed with a bang. Except for the brilliant white beam of light from the head-torch, he was standing in total darkness. He patted the shoulder holster under his coat and took out the Glock. He unloaded it and reloaded it and put it away. More out of habit and doing the right drills than anything. Maybe he was just buying himself some time. He wasn't afraid of dark enclosed spaces per se, but the idea of descending down into the sedimentary rocky depths of an eighteenth century city also didn't fill him with joy. He heard the rat scurry behind him and he spun. Hate rats. He turned and shone the beam and watched it dive into the hole and down the stairs.

"Lead the way, why don't you," he said and followed the rodent into the darkness. He could see his breath in the white light as he descended the steps. It was a long, roughly hewn, and narrow set of stairs that took him down around eighty feet. That's deep, he thought. He switched the head-torch off and took a knee. He waited, silent, in the darkness. At first his vision swirled with the remnant of colours from the light, then his eyes adjusted to the blackness. It would take a few more minutes for optimal night vision.

The catacombs were on three levels, most of it uncharted. The air was stale. He heard the dripping of water and distant echoes in the long stone tunnel. Some of the caves had been used as bunkers in the war.

In the distance, Hunt thought he saw a faint light trail to follow. He was looking for one of the Soviet bunkers. He was early. His curiosity had gotten the better of him. That, and the boredom in the damp, near empty, safe house made this excursion seem like a night out in comparison. He got to his feet and moved slowly forward. His footsteps crunched under the loose stones and dust of the uneven surface. He put his hand out and touched the cold stone wall. He heard his breathing in his ears as he listened out for sounds in the distance.

Hunt took careful, slow, exaggerated steps and moved towards the dim yellow lights. He wasn't worried about anyone behind him, but there were so many entrances all over the city and so many adjoining passages and caverns that people could be moving unseen and unheard in the darkness on different levels, above or below him. He got closer to the lights. They were yellow bulbs in metal casings and placed every ten or fifteen feet along the passageway.

Hunt was impressed by the choice of location for the dead drop. There was no mobile phone signal this far under the city. No satellite or thermal imaging capability. And, crucially, no closed circuit cameras.

Hunt heard a noise. Footsteps. He pressed his back up against the wall and moved forward on the balls of his feet. He stepped light-footed and fast. Then he saw a figure and panicked and reached for the pistol. "Bloody hell," he said under his breath as he realised it was only a mannequin wearing a Soviet gas mask and opal coloured raincoat.

"Scared me half to death."

He took a deep breath. The mannequin was placed in front of a set of rusted metal gates. He pulled out the pistol anyway and extended it out to his front. He stepped past the metal gates and into the old bomb shelter. Hunt was careful to watch his back. He didn't want to be locked behind the iron bars. He cleared the room. There was a table with old Soviet digging tools and memorabilia. Behind one of the dummy mortars, below a faded propaganda painting of a Soviet soldier, was a thick, clear plastic file. It was conspicuously out of place. Inside the file he could see a padded yellow envelope.

Just then he heard something behind him. He leapt forward and grabbed the folder. He made his way out of the bomb shelter and saw a shadow disappear around the corner to his right and he heard the crunch and echo of multiple footsteps to his left and then the low hiss of someone swearing to themselves.

"Screw this," he said and turned right. A firefight in a tunnel would be bad news for everyone involved. Even bullets that missed him would ricochet. The sound from the blasts would be deafening and disorientating. Too late.

The red beam of a laser sight crisscrossed in front of him. Hunt side-stepped and ducked and a flutter of rounds from a suppressed sub-machine thumped into the soft rock walls behind him. He heard the hushed, urgent shouts of men behind him. Was he followed? Hunt ran down the corridor.

The dim lights ended and he was in a dark section again. He crouched and stopped and waited. There were sounds behind him. Then something to his front. The squeak of leather and patter of rubber soled shoes. His breathing was fast and his senses heightened. Confined spaces and bullets.

He moved towards the sound. The tunnels branched off in different directions. *Eeny-meeny-miny-moe.* He went right. The passage was almost black. It seemed like the room opened up into a cavern. He stood up straight. It was definitely a bigger space, the air was colder, less stale. He heard breathing. He wasn't alone.

"Who's there?" he said. He flicked on the head torch and saw the figure of a girl with shiny-blonde bobbed hair. She ran and ducked out of the far end of the room. "Damn it," Hunt said and switched the light off. There were shouts behind him. Someone said, "This way!"

American accents. Hunt followed the girl. He entered another dark room and he smelled her perfume. She shrieked as he grabbed her and put his hand over her mouth, "Shhhh," he said into her ear. "I'm not going to hurt you." She struggled and kicked out. She was slender and wore tight-fitting leathers, like a motorcycle rider would.

"Get off me," she hissed. "Let go!"

Hunt loosened his grip.

"Was it you," he said, "That left this for me?" If she had, she wouldn't need to see to know he was holding the file.

"They followed you," she said.

"No," Hunt said. "They knew where I was going. They were waiting for me to grab it, which means you told them, or they found out from someone else."

"I didn't tell them," she said. Hunt let her go. She didn't try to run this time. They heard a noise behind them. Hunt lifted his finger to his mouth. They were like moles, using sensations more than sight.

"Do you know a way?" he whispered. He felt her shake her head. Then he heard a clink and a rattle. Something metallic. It banged and bounced off the stone walls and footsteps moved away from them. She grabbed his hand in fright and he felt her cold slender fingers.

"Grenade!" Hunt said and pulled her away. They ran head down to the far end of wherever they were going. Hunt turned the head torch on. He pulled her around a corner and the sound of the heavy thump of the hand grenade tore through the tunnels. His ears were ringing and dust and smoke billowed around them.

"Come on," he said, coughed and pulled her up. They heard voices behind them. Hunt killed the light. They ran. They went about fifteen feet before Hunt's foot caught on something. He tripped and fell and she piled on top of him. They slid and rolled down some sort of ramp and then splash they were in the darkness of an underwater lake kicking and gasping for air. The sound of the water splashing echoed around them. Hunt heard a shout and a man with a light came nearer.

"How long can you hold your breath for?" he asked her.

"What? I - I don't know."

"Do you know the term 'suck and chuck'?"

"What? No!"

He took a deep breath and pulled her under with him. She writhed and yanked at his arm, but he pulled her deeper and swam for the back of the cavern. He heard the gunshots from under the water and the rounds penetrated the water around them. There was a beam of light above them and bullets hit the water and spun past them as they dived and swam. The water was cold and felt oily. It took away his breath and burned his chest. The girl tried to fight him and pull herself to the surface, but he knew they'd be shot. He dragged her to the back of the cave and turned his head torch on. He was running out of air. He felt along with his hand and found a cave or a crevice. He pulled her through and they both burst to the top and sucked in air and Hunt shone the light on the walls. They were in another room. He didn't know how hard it would be for the men to find it. They needed to get out and get away.

CHAPTER TWENTY-FIVE

Hunt pulled himself out of the water and then lifted the girl out. He sat on the dry stone floor coughing. They both shivered.

"We've got to go," he said.

The girl said nothing. She got up and felt along the wall for an exit. She turned to him in the dark and said, "Are you coming or not?"

She was English and not what Hunt was expecting. She sounded like she was from London, but definitely South East England. Hunt clocked it, but didn't mention it. Not the right place or time.

Water dripped off him as he stood. He pulled out the pistol and followed behind her. She seemed to know where she was going. She led him around corners and down small alleyways in the maze of tunnels and caves. Eventually they came to a metal ladder leading to the surface outside. She climbed ahead of him and braced and struggled as she pushed up on the metal sheet cover. He watched her in the dim light. Her hair was wet, but Hunt didn't think it was real, she was wearing a wig. A disguise. It was too blonde, too well concealed. The leather trousers were tight and form fitting on her.

She didn't wait for him to join her at the top of the ladder. The metal sheet slammed shut and he heaved to get it open. She was already walking away from him when he emerged and said, "Hey! Wait. We need to talk ..." He jogged to catch up to her. She huffed like an annoyed teenager. He was soaked and freezing and was sure she was too. They needed to get out of the cold before they got hypothermia.

She stopped and turned and looked distinctly unimpressed.

"Where are you —" Hunt stopped talking. He recognised her.

"Urgh," she grunted and turned to walk away.

"Wait," he said.

"We need to get out of here."

Hunt was struck dumb. He started to feel anger and confusion.

"You aren't even going to talk to me?" he asked.

She stopped walking and faced him.

"I was trying to protect you, Stirling. Like before. I disappeared, didn't I? I got out of it."

"Without a word ..."

"To protect you!"

"Did you tell them where I'd be?" he asked.

She scoffed and turned and started walking again. He had to pick up a brisk pace to catch up.

"I knew this was a bad idea," she said under her breath as she pulled out a set of keys. She walked across a dark, empty parking lot to a black Kawasaki Ninja sport bike. She unlocked the chain holding the helmet to the handlebars and put it on.

"Where are you staying?" she asked him.

"A safe house."

"Not one Louis set up for you?"

"Yeah," Hunt said.

"You can't stay there. Those guys will be looking for you."

"Who were they?"

"How should I know?" She put the key in the ignition and swung her leg over the seat. "A guy like Louis has been playing both sides for so long I doubt he even remembers which side he started on, or cares."

She turned the key and the engine sprang to life. Hunt stood there soaking wet, shivering-cold, and holding the plastic envelope while the motorcycle sat in a high idle.

"Well," she said above the engine. "Are you coming or not?"

He smiled. Same old Robin. If that was her real name. He knew her as Robin Adler. She'd sat next to him when he'd completed the initial test for MI-6. She'd tried to seduce him during the selection and training for Section Seven. And then, she'd just disappeared. Hunt hadn't seen her for almost five years and now she turns up in Odessa as his contact for a dead drop. Was she still working for MI-6? And, if she was, why was she holed up in the Ukraine doing dirty work for a piece of slime you find under your shoe like Louis Trois?

He didn't know what to think, or who to trust. She revved the bike. He shook his head again. He was soaked. Any longer out in the freezing air and he might as well just lie down and die. He tucked the file down his trousers and climbed on the back and put his hands on the passenger bars.

She blasted the bike down the empty streets. The wind was freezing and blew in his face and his eyes watered. They zipped south, she doubled backed on herself, and performed some standard, but well executed manoeuvres to shake any tails. Hunt was impressed. Then, she raced down the back of a tall building with a park on one side and, without warning, ducked the bike down a concrete ramp and into an under-ground parking garage. The sound of the engine was monstrous in the enclosed space. She revved it and rode right

173

into an open garage. She shut the engine down, climbed off and took out the keys. She waited for him to leave and then pulled down the garage door. She took the helmet off and glanced at him. Her expression had softened a bit. There'd always been something between them. Hunt couldn't tell if, in the past, it was real from her side, or just part of the act to 'turn' him and get him onside. To see if she could make him her asset. She reminded him of Kate, his ex-fiancée and that was his soft spot.

She led him to a bank of lifts. They didn't speak. When they got into the lift she leaned back against the mirror and looked at him, "I'm only doing this because I owe you one," she said.

"Louis doesn't know where you live?"

She stood up and shook her head, "No, and I wouldn't bring you here if he did."

"You think those goons know about the safe house?"

The lift came to a stop and doors opened. She walked out and said, "There's nothing safe about it. Forget it now, anything you had in there is ransacked and gone."

"Why do you do it?" Hunt asked as she opened a heavy black door to a penthouse apartment.

"Take your shoes off," she said and pointed to a plastic tray in the corner. He did as he was told. The apartment was big and decorated in soft white tones contrasted with black and silver. The living room had a large three-seat sofa along the back wall and a view looking north east over Odessa. Hunt gave a low whistle. The opposite wall was floor to ceiling monitors and hardware. It was an impressive setup. Now he knew why she could do what she could do. A white cat meowed and came to rub herself against Hunt's leg.

"She likes you," Robin said and picked the cat up and cuddled her. Hunt thought of Flea back in London and wondered how he was getting on. Miserable bloody stray. He missed him.

"Shower's through there," she said. "Help yourself. There should be spare towels and some clothes you can wear until yours are dry."

"Thanks," Hunt said and stood there silently for a moment. He went to have a hot shower and put his clothes on one of the towel racks.

He came out of the spare bedroom with bare feet, wearing chinos with no belt and a too-tight woollen knitted jersey. His hair was still a bit wet, but he was warm, finally. Robin was still at her computer. She'd showered and changed into a fluffy white robe. Her cat sat on her lap and she hugged it and held it close and kissed its head.

"Why do they want to kill you?" she asked. He stood in the open space of the adjoining passage for a moment.

"I was hoping you were going to help me with that," Hunt said. She looked up at him out of the corner of her eyes. That same naughty look he recognised from the Kill School.

"You don't know?" she asked and then said, "Maybe I can. Do you still have the files?"

Hunt motioned to the bedroom.

"Here, I'll show you," she said. The cat jumped off her lap and went to Hunt and pressed her body against his shin. Robin smiled and tapped on her keyboard. Hunt came over and stood behind her. It was surreal. He smelled the clean freshness of her hair and robe. He turned and looked out of the windows. The view over Odessa was spectacular in the night sky.

"Are you happy here?" he asked.

She concentrated on the screen and frowned.

"Why'd you do it?" she asked and then turned to look at him and said, "Not that it's any of my business, but why. I never pegged you for that sort."

"What sort?"

"Killing your assignment."

Hunt frowned and shook his head.

"There's a video, Stirling." She hit play. The black and white video started playing. Hunt running up the stairs. Standing over General Patrick.

He clenched his fists. "It's fake," he said. "I didn't kill him. A blonde woman did."

Robin squinted and went back to the screen.

"That's not what the Intelligence Director is saying. They're saying it was you."

Hunt shook his head. "It's a frame. I'm being put in a frame."

"Why though?" she asked.

"Because of this ..." Hunt said and pulled out the watch. "I don't know the reason or the significance. All I know is that Patrick gave this to me for safe keeping, moments before he was killed. The blonde walked out with his briefcase. Whatever she was looking for, they thought it would be with his business things. His diplomatic case."

Robin put out her hand and Hunt looked at it for a moment.

"Let me see," she said.

Hunt relented and put the diamond encrusted watch in her hand. She studied it and turned it over and looked at it from different angles.

"How do you open it?" she asked.

"I don't know."

"What's this?" she pointed to the inscription.

"Anniversary present," Hunt said.

"Have you tried to open it?"

Hunt shook his head. "Not yet."

"We should try!" she said excitedly. Her eyes lit up like it was her present. Hunt smiled. It was a nice scene. Playing house for a moment. Hunt took back the watch.

"Maybe later."

She pouted. "Suit yourself."

"Why don't you walk me through what you found ..."

"Sure," she said and turned back to the keyboard. "They're after you, you know? They think you did it. There are warrants out for your arrest. Those guys there tonight, they weren't police. You've been burned ..." she turned to look at him, "Like me."

"What happened to you," Hunt asked. "After the Kill School and everything ..."

She shook her head. "Another time."

"I found something else," she said. Her eyes glinted. It was a I know your secret look. Hunt was confused.

"I'm surprised they let you in at all ... you must have been a good liar, or covered it up really well but, I found it," she said as she typed rapidly and seemed very pleased with herself. Vindicated.

"What are you talking about?" Hunt said, almost finding it funny. He had no secrets.

"About your mother ..." she said.

"What?" Hunt shook his head. "She's dead, so, what're you talking about?"

Her face froze and stayed like that. She looked at him for some time. Then at the ceiling. She turned back to the keyboard and said, "When did she die?"

The moment flashed in his mind. The panga in his father's back. Kabazanov's eyes. The shattered glass.

"Because, if you say the nineteen-eighties, she didn't. She's in the system until two thousand-and-four. Then, she disappears."

She looked at him. Hunt closed his eyes tight and scratched the back of his head. He felt dizzy and wanted to sit. He shook his head and opened his eyes and looked at her and sighed.

"I'm sorry, I thought you knew," she said.

He shook his head slowly.

"No ... I've believed she was dead since I was young. Someone said she was alive, or at least, didn't die, but they weren't trustworthy."

"I'm your second source then."

"How do you know?"

"Her name changed and her biographical details were edited, but it's definitely her." Robin pulled up a scan of a redacted and stamped SVR file.

"I don't believe it," Hunt said. There she was. A black and white picture, but a son never forgets his mother's face. He could have picked her out of a crowd right now.

He shook his head, "She's alive?"

Robin nodded. "Well, we know she was alive until two thousand-and-four."

"Why, what happened then?"

"She fell off the grid and hasn't resurfaced yet," she said. "Theoretically she could be dead, but no records, and nothing suggests it."

"What happened in oh-four?"

"They closed the schools," Robin said. "State School Four in Kazan. Sparrow school. They disbanded and the trail runs cold."

Hunt stood silently staring at the screen. His breathing was deep and focussed. It's true. She's alive. Aslan Kabazanov was telling the truth. He was struggling to get to grips with the significance. The man he killed was telling the truth. The man who'd sent him to do it was a liar.

He saw Robin swear silently to herself and then look him in the eyes.

"Stirling, I'm so sorry, I thought you knew, I thought you must know. How could they hide that from you? I thought I'd found an intriguing little secret, well, it was a secret, but I didn't know it was a secret from you." Her eyes glistened and her lower lip quivered.

"It's okay," he said and put his arms out. She got off the chair and came over and hugged him. She was warm and soft and it felt comforting. It calmed him down. He hadn't had a proper hug in ... he didn't even know.

"What're you going to do?" she asked him. Her voice was muffled by his chest as she spoke. He looked down at her.

"Let's open the watch," he said.

CHAPTER TWENTY-SIX

"How?" she asked him.

"Don't you think it's strange?" he asked.

She let go of him and stepped back and looked quizzically at him.

"An anniversary present at Christmas time? I've spent every day with Patrick for the last six months. He's not random. You know? He's - was - a British Army General. He was precise. Methodical. Uncreative. I feel like the anniversary message was a cover or a code."

"Okay, so how do we open it?"

"Seventh of July," Hunt said. She furrowed her brow. "That's his anniversary."

She pulled a chair over for him and they sat down at her desk. She pulled the desk lamp down so the light shone on Hunt's hands. He held the watch in the light and diamonds glinted. He pulled out the pin on the side of the watch. One click to change the time, two clicks to change the day, three clicks change the month. He pulled it out as far as it would go and rolled it between finger and thumb. The day counter changed until it was set to seven. Then he clicked it out once more and changed the months. He set it to the seventh of July. They looked at the watch and waited expectantly. They glanced at one another. Nothing. Nothing happened. Hunt laughed. "Well, that's me out of ideas."

He sat back in his chair and looked at the ceiling, thinking. He counted silently on his left hand, one, month, two, date, three, time. "Month, day, time," he said. "What if it was set to a specific time?"

She thought about it, "I don't know about watch mechanisms, but it would make sense if all the gears and wheels had to work together to open it."

"Going train."

"Excuse me?"

"That's what it's called."

"Oh, excuse me, Mister Copernicus."

Hunt looked at her blankly.

"Didn't he make watches?" she asked.

"I don't know," he said. "Should we get back to trying to open this up?"

They both looked back at the watch. The light shone off the glass and silver. "You know what the parts of a watch are called, but you don't know one of the world's most famous watchmakers," she said quietly. Hunt glanced at her.

"I know he stole the idea that the planets revolved around the sun," Hunt said. "I didn't know he made watches, okay? If you'd said Hublot, I'd have known."

He gave her a wry smile and she grinned and asked, "What time do we set it for?"

Hunt turned the knob and the minute hand spun. "I don't know, what about twelve?"

"A.M. or P.M.?"

Hunt just shook his head.

"What?" she said and slapped him lightly on the shoulder. "That was a good one!"

"There, twelve on the seventh of July."

They both looked at the watch and waited. Robin was anxious. Hunt's brow furrowed. Nothing. It was steady. Dead. No change. Robin suddenly grabbed his arm, she sat upright, eyes wide and stared straight ahead and said, "It's a mechanism, right?"

"Yes."

"So, it must be mechanical to work. Don't set it to midnight, or twelve, on the seventh. Set it to one minute to midnight on the sixth. Then, when it ticks forward, the mechanism will engage."

Hunt nodded. It made sense. He adjusted the dial. "Okay," he said. "I am clicking it shut now, eleven fifty-nine."

They waited. The second hand started to tick. Sixty seconds. After this, Hunt was truly out of ideas. Tick, tick, tick. Robin's hand squeezed his arm and her nails dug into his forearm. They both sat forward and peered at the watch face. Tick, tick, tick. The second hand ticked up to twelve and the date changed to the seventh and silently and precisely the back of the watch came open.

"Oh my God," Robin said. "It worked!"

"You're a genius," Hunt said. She let go of his arm.

"Look inside!" she said urgently.

"Here," he said and handed her the watch. "My fingers are too fat."

"Butchers hands," she said and took the watch.

"Yeah, they're good for a few things," Hunt said.

She gave him a sideways look and leaned forward and held the back of the watch under the light. The rear had popped out on little hinges. She held it delicately on either end between finger and thumb and tried to twist it. "I don't want to damage it," she said quietly.

"Maybe it slides," Hunt said.

"I'll try," she slid the back of the watch up and it came out smoothly. She turned it over in her hand and then placed it down. She looked into the back of the watch. "I don't see anything," she said.

"Do you have a magnifying glass or something?" Hunt asked.

They both leaned in to look at the back of the watch. The mechanism was working. The watch ticked away. It was stuck at twelve o'clock on the seventh of July.

"What am I looking for?" she asked.

Hunt shook his head. "I have no idea." There must be something though, he thought. Surely General Patrick wouldn't have gone to all this trouble for nothing at all.

"What's that," she said and pointed.

Hunt took the watch and leaned in and squinted. There, on one of the wheels was stamped, or engraved a 'Ghb'. "There are sequences of letters and numbers, uppercase and lowercase, on the wheels and gears," Hunt said. He sat back and looked at Robin and she stared at him. "Some sort of code?"

"We need to write them down," she said.

"How do we know what sequence they're in?"

"We could reset it to twelve on the seventh and then see what sequence they come out with."

THEY DID IT. It was painstaking work. Her cat had long gone to curl up by herself on the sofa. Finally, Hunt sat back and tilted his head and rubbed his eyes. "That's it I think," he said and yawned.

Robin was counting the number and letter combination by moving the tip of the pen along the row and silently moving her mouth. She put the pen down and said, "Fifty," and shook her head.

"What is it?"

"It's a key," she said.

"A key to what?"

She dropped the corners of her mouth and shook her head.

"Something important, but there is no real way to tell without more information."

"How do you know it's important?" Hunt asked and sat forward.

"You mean besides the fact that it was stored on randomly inscribed wheels in the back of a luxury watch that you need a code, itself, to open?" she said. "How about the fact that the man who had it is dead, killed not by you apparently, and that the only other person who had it in their possession is being framed for murder and is the target for assassination himself."

"You don't believe me?" he asked.

"You're missing the point, Stirling. It doesn't matter what I believe. Those are the facts. Whatever this is, and it looks like a very sophisticated decryption key, people want it and they are willing to kill to get it."

"How do we work out what it's for?"

"This is only the first layer," she said. "This will translate into a hexadecimal code."

"Hexa-what?"

"This code will be fed into a translator and will then be converted into a different string of numbers and letters called a hexadecimal code. Judging by the length it'll be seventy-two hex-characters. Which means a two hundred-and-fifty-six bit key."

"You're losing me," Hunt said.

"We're talking about military grade encryption," she said. "Unbreakable."

They sat quietly for a moment.

"I'll try and explain it another way. If fifty supercomputers could check a billion-billion keys per second, if such a device could even be made, it would still take three times longer than the universe has existed for, in its entirety, to solve it. I mean, a quantum computer would drastically reduce the time, but even that would take longer than the universe has existed."

"So, a long time then?" Hunt said.

"This isn't funny," she said, "this is serious."

"How long has the universe existed?" Hunt asked.

"Almost fourteen billion years," she said. "Not a million. Billion. A million seconds is twelve days. A billion seconds is thirty-one years."

Hunt was quiet, trying to let it sink in.

"Whoever made this," she said. "Didn't want it to ever be broken. The only way to decrypt the encryption is to have this key. Whoever has it has access to something that someone didn't want anyone else to have access to."

They were quiet.

"But we have no idea what it is for?" Hunt asked.

"No, but we can guess. General Patrick was close to the Joint Chiefs of Staff. The National Security Agency has been working on encryption for decades. They've invested billions. There has been talk of a system that would encrypt everything on the internet. If you could do that, everything would be protected, unless you had something like this key, which would allow whoever had it to see everything on the internet. All the most secret information that the deep state doesn't want anyone else to see."

"Knowledge is power," Hunt said.

"Absolute power."

They both looked at the watch.

"So, what do we do?" Robin asked.

Hunt shook his head.

"This is our insurance," Hunt said. "As long as only we

know where it is, we're alive. As soon as they know where it is, we're dead."

"They'll never stop."

"So we destroy the paper," he said and pointed to the key. "Close up the watch and put it somewhere safe," he said.

Robin looked worried.

"I shouldn't have brought you here," she said and put her head in her hands. Hunt sighed.

"It's too late for that now," he put his hand on her shoulder.

"There's nowhere safe enough that we can put it," she said and looked him in the eye. She looked afraid.

"Who else knows you helped me?" Hunt asked.

"Only Louis, but he doesn't know who I am. At least, I don't think he does."

"Which means anyone could know."

"For the right price," she said. "I'm arguably too valuable to him to give up, but you never know."

"Louis only knows what he knows - that people are after me and where I am. Nobody is going to tell him about this key," Hunt said.

Her bottom lip quivered. "I'm sick of running, Stirling. I'm so tired of it."

"Me too."

"So what are you going to do?" she asked.

"Put an end to it."

She touched his hand.

"Put the people who're chasing us in the ground," he said.

"Where are you going to go?"

"Russia," he said. "To follow the only clue we have."

"What about this?" she motioned to the diamond encrusted watch lying on the desk.

"We put it back together and keep it as an insurance policy. If anything happens to me, you send it to this address and give it to this man."

Hunt took the pen and scribbled down: Gerald Soames, Director in Intelligence, Secret Intelligence Service.

"Him," she said. "Are you sure?"

"He's the only one who would know what to do with it."

"Yes, but can you trust him?" she asked.

Hunt furrowed his brow. If he couldn't trust Soames, then there was no-one on earth left for him to trust.

CHAPTER TWENTY-SEVEN

Hunt stood with his back to the smooth flowing, icy-black Volga River and looked up at an abandoned building. It looked like a once-proud stately home. He could see his breath in the freezing air.

Hunt looked down at the old picture he held in his gloved hand and then up at the building like he was trying to match someone's face to their passport photograph.

He was standing outside of, and looking up at, the building that used to be Kazan State School Number 4. The last place his mother was known to have been, almost a decade ago.

It had a wide set of stairs that ran almost the length of the building and led up to six pillars in the Greek style. The Romans borrowed from the Greeks and everyone trying to create an empire had since made round pillars a staple of their architecture. A symbol of strength and stability and power.

In the photograph the building looked alive, more vibrant, and a place you'd feel honoured to enter every day. Now, it was boarded up. Tiles were missing from the roof. The paint had peeled and moss grew on the window frames. A layer of snow lay undisturbed on the sloped roof and on the stairs and covered the lawn at the front. Maybe he'd find answers inside. He doubted it. What was he hoping for? A steel filing cabinet of records and documents. Something to tell him where she'd gone. Another clue to follow so he could end this.

He climbed the stairs and stood outside the giant double doors. They were made of thick wood, carved with intricate detail, and they were faded. They needed a coat of varnish. The wood was starting to rot. There was a thick chain and padlock on the outside, so he walked along the colonnade. The tall windows were sealed shut with plaster board and covered in graffiti. Hunt went around the side of the building. He checked the angles and the view from the street. As he walked along the row of windows he used his gloved hand to pull and test the plaster board. One of them was loose. He stuffed the picture in his breast pocket and forced his fingers on both hands under the prefabricated wooden sheet. He gave it a pull. He heard a crack. He glanced over his shoulders again and pulled harder. It bent and the nails came part way out. One more heave and the entire bottom corner of the plasterboard pulled back and snapped with a loud crack. Hunt threw the piece down and removed the rest of it. By the time he was done he was feeling warm and he was a bit out of breath. He climbed onto the window sill, and used his fist to break the pane of glass closest to the middle of the sash window. He unscrewed the brass knob and climbed down. The window opened. He had one last check to make sure he hadn't been seen and heaved himself up onto the sill and through the window. He was sure to close and lock it again. The room he was in was dark and dusty. His eyes adjusted to the gloom and he saw an old blackboard on the wall and stacks of metal framed desks and chairs all pushed up at the back. It was a classroom. His nose itched and he held it closed between finger and thumb to stop himself from sneezing. He took his hand away and wiggled his nostrils until he was sure he wouldn't sneeze. He needed to find the main offices or a basement storage facility. Hunt decided to start at the basement and work his way up.

The corridor was gloomy and echoey. He heard water dripping somewhere above him. He turned left and made his way to the front door. The design of the building looked like two floors centred around an open courtyard. His footsteps echoed loudly against the stone and tiled floor. It felt colder inside than outside. He rounded a corner and saw the tall double door entrance. It opened up onto a hall and a high, arched ceiling with doors running off in three different directions. In front of him was a stained glass window above another set of wooden doors. It looked like a large ballroom or dining room. He figured, if it was a dining room, the kitchen would be nearby and it might lead to a basement storage of some kind.

The dining room was dark. Curtains were drawn. His shoes scraped and knocked against the wooden floor. Something didn't feel right. He stopped walking and as his eyes adjusted to the dull light. He heard a noise.

"Who's there?" he said. His whole body was tense. He felt like a rabbit in a hunter's sights. He heard a switch flick on the wall behind him and a single large bulb hanging from the ceiling came on.

Hunt saw a woman sitting cross-legged on a chair directly in the middle of the room. She wore a red leather overcoat that matched her bright red lipstick and her platinum blonde hair reflected the light above her head.

Hunt was glued to the spot. She uncrossed her legs and

stood up. As she walked forward she indicated the man behind Hunt with a black-gloved hand. Hunt glanced at him quickly over his shoulder. Heavy-set thug in a leather jacket that was a size too small.

"Don't try to run, Stirling," she said. Her accent was Russian.

"I recognise you," he said, then it clicked. "Safe flight from London?"

It was the woman who'd killed Patrick. Three more thugs stepped out from the shadows. She walked right up to him and said, "Where is it?"

He just looked at her blankly. He'd recovered his composure now. She reached into his coat and pulled the Glock from its shoulder holster. She held it in both hands and looked at it. Then passed it to the barrel-chested thug.

"How did you find me?" he said.

"Does it matter?" she asked and pulled out a handheld mirror and checked her lipstick in the reflection. She snapped it shut and put it away and looked him in the eyes.

"You have something I need," she said. "If you give it to me, I will let you go." She paused for effect. "If you won't give it to me, I'll take you to him and you'll be killed."

"I don't have it," he said. It was simple and the truth. Her eyes grew wider and a small smile formed in the corners of her mouth, she turned from him and paced. Hunt stayed where he was.

"So you do know what I'm talking about, yes?" She spun on her heels and faced him. Hunt glanced over his shoulder at the thug who was standing too close behind him. He could smell his bad cologne and worse breath. She lifted her chin and the man stepped back.

"Don't worry," she said. "These meatheads can't understand you. They only do what I instruct. Now, you are going to tell me where it is ..."

"Why would I do that?"

"Because without it, we're both dead."

"I'm not afraid to die."

"Maybe not, but wouldn't you rather live?"

Hunt said nothing. He was thinking about ways to escape. He wanted to keep her talking. Could he overpower the guys behind him and get his gun?

"What's your name?" Hunt asked.

She stopped moving and smiled and said, "Natalia."

"What is it for, Natalia? The code."

"You don't know?" she said. She was intrigued. She lifted her hand to her mouth and paced in front of him again. He stayed where he was, in case one of the guns trained on him got jumpy and fired. "Why did you run, if you didn't know what it was?"

"I don't like being set up."

She nodded. She looked like she was weighing up the pros and cons and decided to tell him.

"It's a decryption key to the newest top secret piece of American encryption software. Whoever has that key controls the information. Whoever controls the information —"

"Controls the world."

"Exactly. Yes."

"And who is it exactly that wants it?"

"Everybody, Mister Hunt, but the man I work for, I won't say his name," she lifted her head to the goon behind him indicating that they would recognise she was talking about their boss. "He's the one who wants it most. He's willing to kill to get it. And in particular," she pointed her index finger at him, "he wants to kill you."

Hunt stood there. Waiting. Thinking. She was thinking too.

"Was General Patrick involved?" Hunt asked. He needed to know if the general had betrayed him. Betrayed the country. She shook her head.

"He wasn't involved with our side," she said.

"Then how did you know about the decryption key? How did you know about the intelligence?"

"Anatoly has someone on the inside. I don't know who it is."

"Anatoly is your boss?"

"Don't say his name," she said and shot him a look.

"He's your boss?"

She nodded.

"Why're you telling me this?" Hunt asked.

She sighed and stepped closer to him. She moved within range of his lips. She ran her hand down the underside of his lapel and whispered, "We may be able to help one another. I can take you to him. In fact, if you won't tell me where it is, I have to take you to him, but it's what we do once you're there that means I rub you ... if you rub me."

"Scratch," Hunt said.

"Whatever you like," she said and looked up at him seductively.

"Why would you do that?" he asked her.

Her face softened for the first time. He saw something under the make-up and the persona. She stepped back.

"You can help me kill him," she said. Her face was serious. Hunt felt she meant it.

"Am I supposed to do that in chains —" Hunt heard rapid footsteps and before he could turn he felt a heavy strike on the back of his skull and sharp pain at the base of his neck. His body collapsed.

"I'm sorry," he heard her whisper.

His vision closed in and the last thing he saw was the bright electric light on the ceiling as he closed his eyes and lay on the cold, dusty, wooden floor.

CHAPTER TWENTY-EIGHT

Hunt came around in the back of a horse trailer. It was covered in hay and mud and smelled of manure. He lay on his side on the cold steel and bounced and shook as the trailer was pulled at speed. Freezing wind blew through the openings in the sides. Two heavyset guards sat on the wheel arches with their arms across their chests trying to keep warm. They wore grim expressions.

One noticed he was conscious and kicked a boot out at his mate and tilted his head towards Hunt. The man looked down at him and smiled perversely. He was enjoying this. There was a sense in the back that even though Hunt was the handcuffed one lying in the muck, they were in the manure together.

"Happy New Year," the guard said to Hunt in a thick Russian accent. It came out as a guttural 'crappy New Year.' It was thick with irony and as he said it they went over a big bump and the guards had to put their arms out to keep their balance and Hunt's body lifted and landed hard on the hard metal surface. The guards laughed and commented on the perfect timing of the joke.

Christ, it was New Year's Eve. Christmas Day was spent

on the run in London. Boxing Day soaking on a stormy beach in France. And now he was in handcuffs in the back of a horse trailer on New Year's Eve. It didn't get much better than this. All he'd wanted to do was hang up his boots while he still could. Now he was in the middle of a global conspiracy to steal American secrets and control the flow of information on the global internet. By the time most people went back to work, he could be in some pit covered in quicklime to aid in decomposition. Or at the bottom of some abandoned mine shaft waiting for a bear or fox to sniff out his rotting corpse. Yeah, it was going to be a great new year.

The trailer slowed down and then stopped. The guards got up and gave him a few light kicks to spark him up and then lifted him. The tailgate crashed down and they escorted Hunt down the ramp. A helicopter waited.

They were on the outskirts of Moscow. Hunt could see the early evening lights from the city as they twinkled in the distance. It wasn't even an airfield. Just a patch of land with a helo landing pad on it. The rotors started to turn and they carried him over to the chopper and bundled him in the back. One of the guys climbed in and lifted him onto the row of seats facing forwards. They left his hands cuffed behind his back and put the seat belt over him and pulled it tight. The guy double checked that he was strapped in tightly and then, leaning in so Hunt could smell his revolting breath again, tapped him on the side of the face and said, "Sleep well." He said it in a thick Russian accent. Then he scoffed and hopped out of the aircraft.

The rotors were at full spin and Hunt saw Natalia climb out of a black Mercedes Benz. The downwash from the blades blew her hair back and lifted her red coat as she walked towards him. She shook her head nonchalantly. She knew everyone was watching her, Hunt included. She climbed in the back and without saying anything put a set of the helicopter's headphones over his ears. She sat opposite him and clipped herself in and put her own headset on and said into the microphone, "We're ready …"

The engine roared and they lifted off the ground. Once they were properly airborne and flying south east, Natalia switched the headset controls, and spoke to Hunt.

"The pilot can't hear us now," she said. "I'm taking you to see him in Sochi. He has a palace there. It was a giant compound built into the side of the mountain on the shores of the Black Sea."

Hunt didn't respond. He didn't know what to say. He was suspicious. Just a pawn in a game where everyone was trying to use everyone else to get ahead, or save themselves, or get one up on one another. Not quite his cup of tea. More the kind of guy to finish some aggro than start it. He didn't care for being put into a position he couldn't control. Even with the engine and wind noise, the silence between them was awkward. He could see it on her face. There was no doubt she was beautiful, but there was something else there too. There was something important she wasn't telling him. Then he said, "You mentioned the name Anatoly. Who is he?"

She shook her head and looked out of the window at the blackness.

"A bad man," she said and her eyes locked with his. "A very bad man. Probably the next Prime Minister of all Russia."

Hunt nodded slowly. Power. And money. But mostly power. A man's power tended to seep away from him when he had a blade sticking out of an artery, Hunt thought.

"Is that what all this is about?" Hunt asked through the headset. His voice sounded far away.

"Power and revenge," she said. "And control. You've been a thorn in Anatoly's side for many years now."

"Me?" he said with incredulity. "How is that even possible, I'd never even heard of him."

She just shrugged and looked back out of the window. He sensed she wasn't going to say more.

"How do you fit into all of this? Why do you work for someone that is such a bad man?"

"I don't have a choice," she said more to herself than to him. She was staring out the window. "One day I will be free." She looked at him. "Hopefully soon. You're going to help me, aren't you?"

"Help you?" He asked and indicated his hands behind his back with a tilt of his head. "You've put me in handcuffs and killed my asset. You're threatening to throw me to the wolves and you want help?"

She shrugged and looked serious and said, "We can live together or we can die together. Anatoly won't stop until he has the decryption key. If you don't give it to him, he will kill you, and if you don't give it to him, he'll kill me too."

"And you're going to help me kill him?" Hunt asked.

She just stared into his eyes, like he was supposed to read her mind. Her face was blank and knowing. It meant something. To Hunt, all he knew was that if he took a shot and missed, he was done for. She might still be okay, or survive, but his life was the one on the line. For her it was a case of 'heads I win, tails you lose'. Hunt couldn't afford to miss.

HUNT COULD SEE twinkling lights out of the window offshore. Lots of boats and yachts of all different sizes.

"What're they doing there?" he asked.

"The fireworks," Natalia said. "It is one of Anatoly's benevolent gestures. Every New Year, he puts on a display. People come from all over ..."

Hunt nodded, unimpressed. He looked the other way and saw the steep white tipped mountains rising up in the distance around the Black Sea.

The airspeed of the helicopter slowed and their altitude dropped. They were preparing to land. Natalia's expressions and demeanour changed noticeably. She became more tense, more serious, and more fidgety. She reached into her top breast pocket and pulled out a small silver key. She unclipped her belt and leaned forward and said, "Open your mouth."

Hunt wasn't sure what to make of it at first.

"For later," she said and pushed her leather gloved fingers into his mouth and dropped the key between his teeth and his cheek. It tasted metallic and dirty. "Don't swallow it," she said unhelpfully as she sat back. Hunt manoeuvred it with his tongue and kept it under his tongue to the left of his mouth.

The chopper gradually sank into the blackness below. It hit the concrete landing pad with a bump and a shudder and came to a halt. The door slid open and Natalia unclipped her belt and climbed out without looking at him. He saw her walk away into the darkness. She was replaced in the doorway by three armed guards in shimmering navy suits, purple ties with matching pocket squares and white shirts. Each man had a Vityaz-SN pointed at Hunt. The Russian equivalent of an MP-5. It had the same trigger and safety mechanism as the AK-74. Russians weren't shy about reusing what worked. Their culture was rooted in a 'if it ain't broke, don't fix it' culture. Everything was to be stored and reused or saved for a later date.

One of the men let his sub-machine gun hang on its sling and swung it around his back. The other two kept their rifles trained on Hunt. The guy climbed into the helicopter with him and unclipped his restraints. He put his hand under Hunt's armpit and guided him out of the chair. Hunt felt his feet hit the hard surface and tried to get a look at his surroundings. He was on the roof of what looked like a large building. Trees swayed in the breeze in the darkness behind him and he saw light glinting off the waters of the Black Sea directly to his front. Hunt saw heavy machine guns planted on all four corners of the upper deck. This guy wasn't taking any chances. The guard guiding him pushed him forward and said, "*Khodit*!"

Hunt moved forward towards the edge. He thought they might throw him off the roof. Then he saw an opening. A set of stairs leading down into the belly of the building.

After he descended the concrete stairs and entered a similarly functional passage of grey-green cement, Hunt heard from behind him, "Stop!"

He stopped and half turned and said, "So you do speak English." He felt a shove in the shoulder telling him not to look back and then a hood came over his head. The surprise made him resist, but once he realised what it was he calmed down. It was like putting blinkers on a horse, or a sack over the eyes of a rhinoceros. He had no choice but to be comfortable without vision. They pulled him forward and he heard them press a button. An elevator door opened and they entered the confined metal box. The door closed and they descended further into the concrete compound.

CHAPTER TWENTY-NINE

When they pulled the black satin hood from his head, Hunt was on his knees in a large elaborately decorated office. There was the crinkling sound of plastic sheeting under him. It was laid out in long strips on the light-coloured herringbone parquet floor. The guards went and stood in the corners of the room with their weapons across their chests. They watched him and waited. One was at the back of the room and the other two were against the walls on either side of him. Above the enormous fireplace was an imposing portrait of Stalin in full military dress. What the hell was going on?

Just then the double floor-to-ceiling doors burst open. A bald man with deeply set eyes that looked like he had alopecia strode in, wearing a brown military uniform. Hunt wondered if he was in some specialist secret police headquarters or something. The bald, skinny man was followed by a brute of a man. He was wiping his mouth with a maroon satin napkin and he pulled at the cuffs of his black dinner jacket. He didn't even look at Hunt. He went behind his desk and shuffled a few papers around and then said, still without looking at him, "You've decided to grace us with your presence, Mister Hunt."

The ogre looked at the skin-covered skeleton for approval of his joke and the skeleton smiled and nodded. The guards were stone faced. Hunt didn't know what to say so he stayed silent.

Then the man looked at him and Hunt saw that he had pockmarks in the excess skin around his bloated neck. He was really unpleasant to look at. Hunt doubted his company was much better.

"You'll have to excuse me if I make this quick, Hunt, my guests are waiting." He checked his watch. "New Years Eve party," he said.

"I can wait ..." Hunt said.

The man was first taken aback and then caught the humour and smiled. He raised his eyebrows and wagged a finger knowingly in Hunt's direction.

"Still with a sense of humour. Very good. Very good. Not for much longer I fear," he spread his arms out towards the plastic wrapped floor under Hunt's knees. "You can see we've prepared for you." Then he stood there impatiently and said, "So?"

Hunt was quiet. "So, what?" he replied.

"Don't mess me around. We both know how this ends. You tell me what I need to know, or you don't, and you die. Or, maybe not, I haven't decided. Maybe I will let you live on as a eunuch. You can be my personal peeled-grape feeder."

The alopecia-suffering skeleton laughed dutifully. Just then Natalia walked in. She tried to ignore Hunt.

"There you are," the ogre said. He switched to speaking Russian.

"You're late to your own interrogation." He extended his arms and Natalia went and kissed him reluctantly on each cheek.

"I'm not late, Anatoly, I've interrogated him already."

"And?" Mints asked and held onto her elbows so she couldn't leave.

"Nothing. Why I brought him here, you might have more success."

He looked past her at Hunt and said in Russian, "Do you speak Russian?"

Hunt looked at him blankly. He switched to English, "She says you won't tell her where the intelligence is. Is this true?"

Hunt lifted his shoulders and shrugged. Mints pushed her to the side and stepped past his desk towards Hunt. He walked up to him and bent down and Hunt got the full visual effect of the bullfrog face. He had big pores in his skin. He had bushy eyebrows, not unlike the portrait glaring down at him, he didn't practice good oral hygiene. His teeth were stained.

"Tell me," he said and leaned in.

Hunt looked away. "It doesn't matter," he said. "You'll never get it."

"So you do know what I'm talking about," Mints stood up. "If it doesn't matter, you may as well tell me."

"If you kill me, it'll end up with the British authorities."

"*Pah*!" Mints scoffed and waved Hunt's comment away. "If I kill you ..." he repeated and laughed. "When ... I kill you. *Eh*?"

"Fine then," Hunt said and shifted on his knees, "When."

"And who is going to receive this piece of intelligence, Hunt? Your boss Mister Soames?"

Hunt didn't say anything. He tried to ignore the question. Mints was glaring at him. His eyes trained on his face like it was a target.

"It is, isn't it?" Mints said and smiled. He glanced at the skeleton and then said, "You really are quite stupid for a spy, Hunt. You've sent the information to the man who stole it in the first place!" He pointed at Hunt and laughed. Hunt's eyes narrowed. He watched Mints closely as he bellowed with laughter. Behind him, Natalia nodded ever so slightly to him. Was she confirming what Mints had said? Mints stopped laughing and looked at him. His face was flushed red. He bent down and grabbed Hunt on the bottom of his jaw and shook his head, "Is it! Is it? Is Soames the man you've sent the intelligence to?"

Hunt clenched his jaw and tried to pull away from the thick fingers as they dug into his teeth and under his neck. Mints stood again, his face even redder. He smoothed the front of his shirt and took a deep breath.

"That means you have no leverage, Mister Hunt. Soames was going to sell the data to me anyway. I decided to steal it first. Now? No matter. You're still finished."

Mints looked at the skeleton and said in Russian, "I'll kill him, *Kretin*, and pay for the code. No problem. I'll rejoin my guests, you see what else he knows. Do it in the basement."

Cretin, Hunt thought, great nickname. What was he going to do now? He was running out of options. *Kretin* nodded and gave Hunt a morbid grin.

"Why?" Hunt asked as Mints prepared to leave the room. The enormous man stopped and looked at him. He was mildly curious.

"Why're you targeting me?" Hunt said.

Mints rolled his eyes and prepared to leave. Then he stopped and turned around.

"That drilling contract in Varrissa, who do you think owned the conglomerate behind the exploration?"

Hunt was silent. He thought it better to let the big man get into the flow of things.

"Russia is not imperialist, Mister Hunt, but I am. We have global ambitions. I can't allow someone like you to continually jeopardise my operations. Years of planning."

"Maybe you need better people," Hunt said.

Mints lifted his hand to his chin and said nothing. Then looked at Hunt again, there on his knees. "You remember Kabazanov? That filthy Chechen thief."

Of course he did. How could he not. Mints poked himself

in the chest and said, "He was one of mine. You think a man like that is easy to find?"

Hunt shook his head. "Next on the list is Gerald Soames," Mints said. "He only sent you after Aslan to get to me, as a bargaining chip, as a way to show me how close he could get to my operations. Someone like Soames, a *slug*, leaving his slime all over my papers, he's useful for a time. He wants to buy an island in the Caribbean; can you believe that? He can use the money he stole from me to buy a smaller island, in a cemetery. As close as he will get." Mints checked his watch. "Now, if you'll excuse me, my guests are waiting."

Something clicked in Hunt's head. He finally saw it. Clear and bright like a cloudless sky. That nagging sensation he'd had. That sense of doom. The desire to get away. That thing that grated like something stuck under his fingernail. Had Soames been working against him from the start? It might explain why something was always going wrong. He decided, there and then that if it was him, he wasn't going to get away with it.

CHAPTER THIRTY

Hunt was taken down to the basement. Narrow face brick corridors leading down dark passages. The cement between the bricks was badly applied and lumpy. The light was dim and came from bare bulbs on the ceiling, Hunt had to duck to stop them hitting him in the head.

The guards walked behind and took him along the musty and damp corridor. When they got to one of the open cell doors, they pushed him into the room, and quickly followed in after him.

One of them grabbed him from behind and pushed him roughly down into a steel chair in the middle of the room. Hunt's wrists were still cuffed behind his back. Once Hunt was seated, the three guards talked amongst themselves. Hunt's Russian was good, but sometimes he lost something in the soldiers' slang. They were discussing who was going to stay with the prisoner. One of them said, "You still owe me drinks from last weekend, Ilyas!"

Ilyas scoffed, "Yes, but your face is uglier than mine so you should stay here with him ..."

"Very funny, you two arseholes, I know I'm not staying so

one of you will come with me and let's go!" the third man said.

Ilyas looked at Hunt. "I wish they'd just kill him and get it over with."

"That's it, Ilyas, you stay with him..."

"I'm not staying, you stay if you're so worried about it."

Hunt watched as all three of them left the room bickering as they went. Ilyas ended up leaving too. He slammed and locked the rusted iron and wood door. Squaddies on New Year's Eve, Hunt thought wryly. He was sure they wanted to party and not babysit him.

The guards' conversation and steps echoed as they made their way down the corridor. Now what, he thought, wait for Natalia to come and save me? Just then, shouts reverberated down the corridor again. It sounded like Kretin had bumped into the guards and he was irate about them leaving Hunt alone. One of the guards came back and peered through the bars, and said over his shoulder, "You see? He's still where we left him. No problem, Kretin, it's okay."

"Don't you dare call me that, only the boss calls me that, you call me sir!"

The cell door slammed against the brick wall as it opened and Kretin, still in full military dress, stepped over the threshold. He glared at Hunt with the sunken eyes and ponderous look of a sociopath given free rein to unhinge his limitless tendencies. Hunt grimaced. Kretin walked up to him and said in Russian, "The boss wants me to find out what else you know ..."

Hunt didn't respond.

Kretin stood looking at Hunt. He looked over his shoulder at Ilyas, the guard stationed outside the door, and shouted in Russian, "Do you speak English?"

"No," the guard shouted back.

Kretin swore under his breath and looked at Hunt, "So, you speak Russian?"

"Very little ..." Hunt said in English.

"If you don't speak Russian, and I don't speak English, how am I supposed to extract the information from you, can you tell me that?" Kretin said.

"We could just be grown-ups," Hunt answered in English. "And agree to disagree."

Kretin furrowed his brow and looked at Hunt deeply and repeated, "Agree to disagree." He seemed bemused.

"Yes," Hunt said. "Why don't we just agree that I'm not going to tell you anything and so you aren't going to get anything out of me, and let's move this along to a natural conclusion, because I'm sick of sitting in these handcuffs and I'd prefer to have a drink at the party upstairs ..."

Kretin stood there looking at him like he was trying to think about what Hunt just said, but Hunt knew this man had no idea what he was saying.

"Hold on," the skeletal saggy-skin faced man said, "I'm going to find someone who can help ..." He banged on the door and the guard stationed outside opened it. Hunt overheard Kretin say, "And don't you dare think about going off duty before I say so." Ilyas didn't respond.

Hunt heard Kretin's shiny brown shoes clipping their way down the slick, damp corridor. Hunt didn't waste any time. He could see the back of the guard's head and kept his eyes firmly fixed on it. He stood and tried to get his hands under his buttocks, but he wasn't supple enough. He had to lie on his back, on the floor, to do it. It was better to be off to the side, out of direct line of sight. He needed a few minutes to get his hands to the front of his body and then to be able to use the key that Natalia gave him.

He took off his shoes by standing on the heel of each one and moved silently out of sight. Hunt got down on his arse and he managed to slide his wrists down the back of his hamstrings. At the same time he was trying to use his tongue to get the key out of his mouth. His muscles in his chest and shoulders and upper back strained against the tightness of the handcuffs and he felt a burning sensation on the skin of his wrists. He was halfway done when he heard two sets of heavy footsteps coming back down the corridor. Damn it, not yet. Not yet.

"Ilyas! Open the door," he heard Kretin say from down the corridor. The keys jangled in the guard's hand and rattled as he fitted it into the keyhole. It was too late. Hunt struggled with all his might. He heard, "Where the hell is he!? I told you to keep your eyes on him!" Kretin was looking through the bars as the guard fumbled with the lock.

"Hurry up! Hurry up!"

The guard finally managed to get the lock open. Hunt screamed in pain at the tension that was going through his arms and shoulders as he tried to squeeze his arms under his legs. He felt that was never going to work, they were about to come in and he was just lying on the cold floor with his arms halfway down his legs. He wouldn't give up.

The door burst open and Kretin entered. Hunt roared in pain as he felt his shoulder wrench out of its socket. The guards came to grab him just as he slid his wrists over his bare feet. They put their hands on his jacket and he jumped up. He concentrated all of his focus on Kretin. Always go for the boss. If they were going to kill him anyway he was gonna make sure to get a few shots in. Hunt bounced one of the guards off with his left elbow and charged at the uniformed Russian.

As he ran at him, Kretin squealed like a piglet on his way home. He put his hands up to protect his bony, rawhide-face. Hunt grunted with intensity and slammed his shoulder into Kretin's jaw.

As he did, he felt his shoulder pop and the dislocated joint slotted back into its socket. Hunt cringed in agony, then the pain became anger. One of the guards lifted the stock of his rifle and brought it down on the back of his head. It was a glancing blow. Hunt turned. He grabbed the guard and put the handcuffs over the back of his head. Hunt pulled the guy's head towards him as he brought his own forehead down on the bridge of his nose.

Hunt head-butted him squarely where his nose connected to his skull, and blood sprayed out in a long stream as the guy collapsed at Hunt's feet. Hunt turned to face the other guard who lifted his weapon and prepared to fire. Kretin was scrambling for the door. Hunt bent quickly in a squat and grabbed the guard at his feet. He pulled the body up in front of him and used the guard as a human shield.

9mm parabellum rounds sprayed from the semiautomatic rifle and Hunt felt the pressure change in the small room as the gunshots rang out. He made himself as small as he could, not through any type of strategy, but just because his mind recoiled in the fear of getting hit. He felt the rounds slam into the guard's body in front of him and he grimaced.

Hunt lifted him up by the collar and charged forward towards the back wall and into the guard with the gun. The guard panicked, but didn't take his finger off the trigger, and the rounds shot up and to the right and slammed into metal bars and the ceiling and ricocheted off the brickwork.

"Stop firing you bloody moron!" Hunt shouted at him as he rammed the guard into the gunman's body. Hunt grabbed the guard's head with both hands. He used the dead guard's cranium like a bowling ball and slammed it over and over into the gunman's head and body.

Hunt saw the submachine gun fall to the gunman's side as he protected his face. Hunt dropped the dead guard's head and lunged at the other guy. Hunt threw wild and swinging double-fisted punches and used his knees hitting into the legs, arms, and body of the guard who'd just tried to kill him.

The guard crumpled to the ground and Hunt stepped on the sub machine gun with his bare foot. Suddenly he realised in the cordite smelling, gun smoke-filled room, that he had a moment to try and free himself. He felt around with his tongue, but couldn't find it. He stuck his dirty, bloody fingers inside his mouth and felt around. The key wasn't there. *Goddamnit*, had I swallowed it? He thought. Where the hell was it?

Hunt froze with his fingers still in his mouth. He smelled of the unmistakable French perfume in the room and, as he was about to turn, he felt the cold end of a suppressor press into the side of his ear.

He couldn't turn properly to see, but heard Natalia's voice.

"What's the matter? Have you swallowed the key?" she said in a mocking, babyish voice.

"What are you doing," Hunt replied. "I thought we were doing this together?"

"You didn't say that you'd arranged for the code to be sent ..."

"What differences does it make," Hunt answered. "I thought you just wanted to get rid of Anatoly?"

"Variables have changed. The key is worth more to me in my position, and then it is easy to get rid of Anatoly."

He was silent for a second.

"So, what happens now?" Hunt asked and glanced down at the twisted bodies lying on the floor around him. Kretin was up against a wall and groaned and lifted a hand to his bloody face.

"I will be the new hero of the hour ..." she glanced at her watch. "And, would you look at that, just in time for a glass of champagne to welcome in the new year too."

She grabbed him by the collar and turned him towards the door.

"We end up in the same position if I kill you down here or Mints does up there. At least this way you've got a chance. Don't forget, yes?"

She said it more as a warning, to stop him thinking about

trying to get one over her down here, and ruin her chances of claiming victory. Typical company girl. Natalia glanced at Kretin over her shoulder as they stepped out of the cell, and said in Russian, "Stop messing around and go and tell the boss that he is needed in his office."

CHAPTER THIRTY-ONE

Hunt was on his knees in the grand office again. Natalia sat on the edge of the desk with her handgun pointing lazily at him. Hunt heard doors slam down the corridor and Mints' violent voice echoing down the marble hallway.

He stormed into the office with a red napkin still tucked into his collar. He noticed it as he entered and yanked it away from his neck. He was followed in by Kretin rubbing his head and two bits of scrunched up, bloody paper towel hanging from his nostrils. One of the guards followed.

"What is the goddamn meaning of this?" Mints ranted. "I asked you to do one bloody thing! One! Not two, or three, or four, only one! And here he is still breathing. What good are you?"

He paced the room and bellowed. His cheeks were flushed. He glared at Hunt. He kept staring. For a long time. It grew awkward. Kretin went to speak and Mints held up his thick hand to silence him. Kretin closed his mouth and looked at his feet.

"Get the Matron," Mints said quietly. Nobody moved. Hunt wasn't sure what he'd said. Mints glanced at the people around him and then screamed, "Get me the Matron!"

Everyone in the office jumped. Natalia, Kretin, and the guard all hurried out of the room to find whoever it was that Mints wanted to see. Hunt was left alone with him. Mints stared out from under his eyebrows at him. He breathed through his open mouth and had flecks of spit in the corners of it like some tired dog.

"You make me very confused," Mints said to Hunt. It was slow and laboured and filled with hatred. Hunt was enjoying it. He was at Mints' mercy, but any small victory felt massive. Anything he could do to disrupt his captor's thinking. If he had more time, he could work out what the hell Natalia was up to.

Hunt didn't reply. He preferred to wait and see what came next. He was still out of breath from the fight in the basement. He needed to conserve his strength. He didn't know when he'd need it next, or when his next opportunity would be.

He heard the *clack-clack-clack* of footsteps on the marble floor outside. Mints looked through the open door with expectation. First came Natalia walking confidently, her red leather overcoat trailing behind her. Then came a woman Hunt hadn't seen before. Kretin brought up the rear. He'd taken the paper towel out of his nose. They all fanned out and the unknown woman stood in front of Mints. She was wearing a black jumpsuit, string of large white pearls, her hair was up. She looked like she'd just been dragged from the New Years Eve party Mints was throwing.

"You wanted to see me," she said quietly to him. It was deferential, but defiant.

Mints extended an arm out towards Hunt, but the woman didn't look.

"I've brought you a present," Mints said. "What's the matter? Don't you recognise him? I've brought you back your son ..."

The woman seemed to stop breathing and closed her eyes.

She turned on her heels, still with her eyes closed. Hunt also held his breath, he was trying to think. Could it be? He was looking up at her. She opened her eyes and her lips pressed firmly together. It wasn't a look that said 'happy to see you'. Her eyes were still. Icy. She held Hunt's gaze. He searched her face for a sign. An emotion.

He had something in his throat. Christ, he thought, did she really have to see me like this. On my knees and begging for my life. If it's really her. She looked familiar. Like something from a dream he remembered. Suddenly, her face softened and she turned to Mints. Her brow was furrowed and she pursed her lips. This was her work face. Concentration and professionalism. Mints ignored her and walked past her and stopped in front of Hunt.

He cleared his throat. "Ahem, I've been thinking about what to do with you, Stirling. By rights I should kill you."

"No," Carmen said. It came out faintly like she had something in her throat. Hunt wasn't sure if Mints had heard. He didn't react.

Carmen went to sit on the desk next to Natalia. They sat close, touching, but didn't look at one another.

Hunt couldn't believe this. Here he was, her only son, being betrayed. He felt like an animal in the zoo. What exactly was going on here?

Mints must have seen the confusion on his face and started to laugh. Kretin joined in. Natalia looked at Hunt blankly. Hunt was staring at the woman Mints' claimed was his mother.

He'd thought she was dead. He'd believed it. He hadn't seen her for over twenty years. Mints was laughing so hard he started coughing and then said to Natalia in Russian, "Did you tell him who you are?"

She shook her head silently.

"She didn't tell you she was your sister?" Mints asked Hunt. Hunt also shook his head. More in disbelief than anything. He was cold, wet, beaten up. He'd just killed a guy in the basement. And this was the happy reunion. His sister giving him up to a mortal enemy with his estranged mother there to watch. He felt the confusion turn to rage.

Carmen glanced sideways at her and Natalia shrugged and said, "Half-sister."

Kretin looked like he was enjoying this. Mints controlled himself and cleared his throat again and stood up straight and smoothed the front of his dinner jacket.

"You see, Mister Hunt, what presents I bring you! A family reunion on New Year's Eve. What could be more tender?"

"You could get me out of these handcuffs so I can thank you properly," Hunt said with a wink and raised his hands up like he was asking for more soup.

Mints lifted his hand to his chin and said "Actually, I've been thinking ... What is the English expression, beat them if you can't join them?"

"If you can't beat them, join them ..." Natalia said, staring blankly at Hunt. Mints turned to acknowledge the help and said, "Yes, if you can't beat them, *join* them. Well, Stirling, you can't beat us. You can't beat me." Mints gestured to the handcuffs and then turned to Hunt's mother and sister behind him. "We have the whole family here, see? Don't you want to join us?"

It was Hunt's time to look confused. He shook his head. It sounded unbelievable to him.

"Why not?" Mints said. "Your people don't want you. They're chasing you for your life."

"They're chasing me because you set me up," he said in a low growl.

"Yes, that is so, but look how well you've done. You show me that you really don't want to die. You show me your will to survive when I look at Kretin's face. So, I said to myself, give him a chance. If you have such a desire to live, I can

215

make you an offer you cannot refuse. Just look, here is your dear mama." He gestured to them in turn. "Your dear sister is here. Here, in this place, you can be with your family. Your true family. Not the bastard English that tried to kill your family. To kill your mama. Kill your father."

"You were the one who tried to kill my father ..." Hunt said. Mints looked smug. He shook his head. "No. No. Think, Stirling." He tapped the side of his head with his finger. "Think! Why would your mother be here with me now, if I was the one who tried to kill her? Tell him," he said and looked at the women.

Quietly, like she was fighting an urge, "It was the English, Stirling."

"I don't believe you."

Hunt felt a knot in his throat again. His mother shrugged and said, "It's the truth."

Natalia moved her arm and put it around her mother. Hunt saw it as Natalia claiming her. She looked at him like he was grounded and she wasn't.

At that moment, Hunt knew he wanted to kill Mints. Mints was looking right at him. He must have noticed the change in his eyes. Hunt's eyes glazed over. Hunt had no cares anymore. Total apathy. He didn't care if he lived or died.

"Listen carefully to me, Stirling," Mints said. "I will only ask you once. An olive branch. I've told you. Soames wanted to kill your mother to get to *me*. Me! It was revenge. And then you escaped the farm. And Soames wanted *you* to get to me again. So he finds you and then, Aslan. Varrissa. You understand? Gerald Soames, Secret Intelligence Service, is my *enemy*, but he is also my customer. It is a Cold War. A personal Cold War between us. We fight, but we also cooperate."

This was all too much for him. It felt like a dream. Had he been knocked on the head? First, his mother was there, some kind of subservient to Mints. A sister he didn't know he had, who'd intended to kill him. And now, Mints was telling him that Soames, his mentor, his father figure, was colluding with the enemy. His whole world was crashing down around him.

"Choose," Mints said.

Hunt realised he would stay as a pawn in the middle of a global game between Soames and Mints. He would stay chained up forever. There was no getting out of this with his freedom.

"You have a choice to make. Now. This second. You can come home, to your roots, here, with us, and do what you were born to do. Or, you can die. You choose."

Kretin pulled out a pistol and cocked it. It seemed like everyone was leaning forward in anticipation, holding their breath, not moving, waiting for him to make his choice.

CHAPTER THIRTY-TWO

Still on the floor, on his knees, looking up at the pockmarked ogre of a man glaring down at him.

His mother shook her head. It was almost imperceptible. Hunt wasn't even sure if he'd seen her do it. Natalia put her head on Carmen's shoulder and gave Hunt a wry grin. Mints smiled. Kretin smiled and stepped forward with murder in his eyes.

"No," Hunt said.

He lifted the pistol. Mints was laughing and suddenly shouted, "Stop!"

"I appreciate the enthusiasm," Mints said. Kretin looked confused and annoyed. He motioned to his broken nose.

"Not yet, not yet, Kretin," Mints said. "This is a special moment. We aren't going to let you take the first sip. This is a fine wine. We must savour it."

Mints looked at Hunt. "You've just signed your own death warrant, Mister Hunt. I get the decryption key either way, remember? I simply have to meet your Mister Soames' price," he said and shrugged.

"You sound like you're still negotiating," Hunt said. "Are you a man of your word, or are you full of *figNya*?"

"Stirling," his mother spoke properly for the first time, saying his name like he was late for supper. "Do as he says and he'll let you live."

She stated like a fact, not like she was a mother pleading with him to join them. He shook his head slowly. He wanted to pretend that she could be an imposter, but there was no doubt in his mind. A son knows. It was his mother, but did she want him to live? She hadn't cared enough to let him know where she was. He felt more alone now than he ever had when he thought she was dead. He had a sister and a mother, but he felt empty.

"Sorry …" Hunt said quietly.

"Yes, yes. You're sorry," Mints said. He looked like he'd just stumbled onto an idea. "Give me your gun Natalia," he said and put out his hand. Reluctantly, Natalia handed him the Sig Sauer P250 with a suppressor attached.

"I don't want to make too much noise before the real explosions start. Let's make this a quick one," Mints said. "I don't want to be late for the fireworks."

Kretin smirked. He was getting his wish.

"Here," Mints said to Carmen Hunt and held the handgun out for her. "If he won't join us, he must be executed."

"*Smert' Predatelyam*," Kretin said. Death to traitors. Mints nodded approvingly and said, "*Predators*, he *must* die. You know this."

Hunt watched his mother as she silently, dutifully, lips pursed with professionalism, she took the gun from Mints. She held Hunt's stare.

She looked down and checked the weapon. Happy it was loaded, she held it in her hands and looked at it for a long time. Mints glanced at Kretin and motioned towards Natalia. Kretin flicked the safety off his Russian-made MP-443 *Grach* handgun and stepped forward crisply and held his arm rigidly straight against Natalia's temple.

"Don't move," Kretin said. "You know I would enjoy nothing more ..."

"Anatoly, you can't be serious. You're really going to do this to me?" Natalia tried to protest.

Mints said nothing.

"Shut your whore mouth!" Kretin commanded. "I'll kill you for fun, bitch."

Hunt saw a change in his mother's eyes. Her cheeks flushed crimson. She was still looking down, but she walked forward. Her hands were steady. Her neck straight. Her chin proud. Mints looked smug, he was about to win.

"You can choose," he said quietly to the matron, "The son dies by your hand, or both of your children can suffer quick deaths. Then it'll be you and me alone."

"Yes," she said quietly. "The son dies by my hand." She seemed focussed. "The son dies by his mother's hand."

Hunt was looking up at her. Could this be happening, after all this time? He went to stand, to reason with her, not on his knees.

"Don't," he said.

"I have to," she said quietly.

Mints came over and pushed Hunt down and held him in place. "Where do you think you're going?" Mints said. "Last chance, Stirling. Don't make your family suffer anymore. Join us ..."

Hunt said nothing. His mother lifted the pistol. It looked big in her hands. She was a tall, slender woman. Athletic, even at her age. Her hand trembled ever so slightly. Was she hesitating? She pointed the weapon at her son's face. Hunt looked into his mother's eyes. He hadn't seen them for decades, but they looked the same as when she'd caress his hair and hum softly to him at night.

"I'm sorry," she said to him.

Mints was nodding. "Yes," he said, "Do it. Do it!"

Hunt saw a flash in his mother's eyes. She looked to her

left with only her eyes. Just then, she lifted the weapon higher, her grip steady now, her face hardened. She lifted it to her right and pointed it at Mints and squeezed the trigger.

She fired three times. Mints' body recoiled. The bullets found their mark. Natalia ducked and swatted Kretin's gun away as he fired. She cried out as the gunshot rang out right next to her ear. She moved away from him and ran as he fired at her. The bullets slammed against the fireplace and mantelshelf and she escaped out of the room. Kretin turned his anger on Carmen.

Hunt was up in a flash. He charged at Kretin. The skeletal soldier squealed again and Hunt barrelled into him and knocked him over Mints' desk. Kretin bundled over the other side, the handgun went spinning away, and Hunt followed. Kretin tried to get up and crawl, but Hunt was on top of him in a flash of rage. He dropped his cuffed hands over the Kretin's head and pulled back and slammed both knees against the back of the Kretin's neck and forced back the chain.

He used the handcuffs as a noose and locked the chain around Kretin's windpipe. Hunt leaned back on the floor. Kretin tried to get his hands inside the metal strapped to his neck. Hunt lay there pulling back on the handcuffs with his face turned away. Kretin flailed, his eyes wide. His feet and legs were the only part of his body to get any purchase and he started to twist. He kicked out wildly. He gurgled and his nose was bleeding again. He was drowning in his own blood. Hunt pulled harder. Kretin's body started jerking.

His mind flashed back to the night of his father's murder. The night Soames had arranged for a depraved KGB agent to orchestrate a gruesome invasion of their farm and kill the whole family. Could it be true?

Hunt strained. Kretin was writhing and trying to fight. He tried to scream and it came out in a gargle, it was no use. He was losing the battle, like a rat in the coiled grip of an anaconda. Finally, blood and snot coming out of his nose and mouth, Kretin stopped writhing. His body went limp and stopped moving. Hunt was breathing hard and pulled the bracelets away from Kretin's neck. He struggled to get out from under the lifeless body. Carmen came over to help and pulled Kretin's dead weight off of him.

"You were about to shoot me then," Hunt said between breaths. He grabbed a pair of Mints' spectacles off the desk and broke the temple piece off the frame. He used the snapped off piece of frame as a pick to open the handcuff locks.

"Trick they teach you at spy school," he said and glanced up at his mother with a wry grin.

"Come on, Stirling, hurry up," Carmen said impatiently, "We have to go!"

"Nearly there," he said. His wrist came loose. "There," he said.

"Very impressive," she said dry and sarcastic. "Let's go!"

"Where?" Hunt asked and took the handgun from her.

"The roof," his mother said. Hunt picked up the pistol next to Mints' body and followed her out.

CHAPTER THIRTY-THREE

Another guard appeared around the corner behind them. He lifted his submachine gun and yelled something. Hunt dropped to a knee and fired a double-tap into the torso. The shout was stifled and the guy dropped. Hunt was up and followed after his mother.

They ran up to the roof. As they climbed onto it Hunt heard a bang and ducked instinctively. Then he saw the bright green flash and heard the hiss of a firework.

"It's starting," she said.

A second later the sky above them was aglow with flashing lights and fireworks. The sound of the explosions was deafening. They were going off right above them.

"Come on," his mother yelled at him and waved him forward towards the helicopter. "You know how to fly?" she shouted as he pulled open the cockpit door.

She ran around the other side. As they climbed in he said, "I used to know, we're soon going to find out." Hunt clipped himself in and flicked the switches and pulled on the headset.

The fireworks display was going off all around them. The engines were whining and the rotors turned.

"Where are we going?" Hunt asked.

"Far from here," she said. "What about Natalia?"

She betrayed me, Hunt thought. She can sort herself out. She made clear whose side she was on.

The helicopter lifted off the roof with a wobble. Carmen braced herself against the door and the centre console. He piloted it straight up. They were about fifteen feet off the ground when Hunt saw Natalia run out onto the roof and raise her hands to her eyes to cover them from the downwash. She waved to them.

"Natalia!" Carmen shouted.

A guard appeared behind her and another. The first one took a knee and fired. The rounds pinged around them.

"Christ!" Hunt said. "It's too late! I have to get us out of here."

"Please, Stirling. Your sister."

"I'm trying ..."

Another guard grabbed Natalia by the back of the hair and pulled her away down and away.

Hunt pointed the chopper towards the Black Sea and flew through the exploding fireworks. He flinched involuntarily as the bright lights fizzed and hissed and thumped against the aircraft. He saw all of the boats below them with people on the decks cheering and waving their arms at them. He looked at his mother, her face serious, concentrating on what was going on outside the helicopter. He focussed on getting as far away from the compound as possible.

He didn't know what to say to her. There was something there. It would take him time. He was so used to the idea that she was dead that in his head she was. She glanced at him.

"Why didn't you try to contact me?" he asked.

She didn't reply immediately.

"It wasn't possible. I was supposed to be dead, remember?" It sounded harsh. Defensive. Then her tone softened,

"Of course I *wanted* to. Of course I wanted you to know. You believe me, don't you?"

He didn't. It sounded like she was saying something she thought he would want to hear. It didn't change anything, even if she wanted him to know she was there all along. The reality was, she hadn't.

"How could I? I was still a Russian agent. As soon as they knew the truth I would be a target again. You would be a target. *And* your sister."

"There's always a choice," he said. "You chose."

Hunt was silent after that. They were flying out over the water now. They'd gotten away. He wondered how Natalia would be. Maybe they would have something in future, if he could forgive her betrayal. He had a sister. A family. The thought was strange to him. So novel. Something he'd never thought before.

"We've all the time in the world now. We can still make up for things we've lost, can't we?" Carmen said suddenly and looked across at him. "When we're free."

"Maybe," Hunt conceded.

Just then there was a shudder and the sound of metal grating. Hunt looked worried.

"What is it?" she said.

"They're shooting at us!" Hunt shouted.

Bullets clanged into the tail boom and rotor.

"Oh, no," he said.

"What!?"

"We're going down," Hunt said.

The helicopter started to spin. He fought hard to control it.

"We're crashing," he said into the mic. "This is *Ansat*-seven-niner-one. Mayday, mayday. I repeat, we are losing altitude approximately ..." he glanced out the window, "Two kilometres south-west of Sochi."

The helicopter was spinning out of control. Hunt's arms

were up against the cabin trying to pin himself down and fight against the spin. The G-force was too much.

"We're going down," Hunt said, fighting the controls. It was going to be cold. The chopper was spinning into the blackness.

"I love you, Stirling," she said. Her eyes were locked on his. She knew.

They hit the surface of the Black Sea. It was like hitting concrete. The front of the cockpit caved in and the glass smashed and water came rushing in. The impact was severe. Hunt hit his head. He was dazed. He touched his head involuntarily and saw blood. The cold shock response made him hyperventilate immediately. Cold water flooded in. He unclipped himself and reached over for his mother. Her head was lolling to the side. She was limp. The water was sloshing in.

"Mum!" Hunt shook her shoulder trying to wake her. He climbed across and wrestled with the harness to unclip her. He was underwater. The cockpit was submerged and it was cold. Hunt felt like someone was sticking him with ten thousand needles all over his body. His brain screamed for air. He kept trying to pull his mother loose from the harness.

Her hair floated up from her head. Her clothing weighed her down and was heavy. Finally, he managed to pull the harness off her. He was trying to fight to get her shoulders out of the strap and manoeuvre her body in the confined space. It was pitch black except for the glow from the instrument panel.

They were sinking. He couldn't handle it anymore. He had to get some air or he would drown. The glass in the windshield was cracked and he twisted himself in the water and kicked at it. He kicked it again and it came away. He forced himself through the windshield and kicked hard for the air. Where was it? He should have broken the surface already. Suddenly, air.

His face broke through the top of the water and he felt the cold wind on his cheeks. He took a few deep breaths and dived down again. He could see the faint white glow of the lights below him. He fought hard to get down. The helicopter was moving further away from him. He kicked hard to swim down and grabbed onto the frame and pulled himself down. He got his hands on her shoulders and managed to rotate her body and pull her towards him. He pulled her limp, pale body through the open windshield. She was weighed down by the outfit, it was heavy, and dragged as he kicked hard. His lungs burned.

They broke the surface. Hunt gasped for air and immediately pulled his mother up and got her head above water. He tried to blow air into her mouth. He couldn't give her cardiopulmonary resuscitation, only try and get air into her lungs. He checked her pulse. His hands were freezing. He couldn't feel anything.

"Come on! Come on!" he blew air into her mouth. It was full of water. He tried to pour it out by twisting her head and tried again. He treaded water and kicked hard to keep them afloat. "Come on, breathe!"

It was dark. He could only see the pale glow of her skin under the moon and stars. She was cold to the touch. He felt for a pulse once more. He was tiring. In water like this, using this much energy, he might be able to last for fifteen minutes. Maybe twenty.

His mother was dead. He was sure of it. He didn't want to believe it. He didn't want it to be true. He'd got to spend just a few minutes alone with her. His teeth were chattering. He was struggling for breath. He sobbed to himself. She was gone. He didn't know how long he stayed with her. He was struggling to hold onto her and keep her body afloat.

Finally, he had to let go. He let her body drift. It floated away from him. The weight of her clothing pulled her down and he lost sight of her under the cold sea.

HE WAS TREADING WATER. His teeth were chattering violently. He'd been afloat for close to thirty minutes. He was pushing the limits of human endurance. He had no coherent thoughts. Hunt was losing consciousness. His heart rate was slowing. His head dropped forward, almost passing out, before he was shocked awake again.

He was barely able to keep himself above water. Hypothermia was setting in. He knew it. It was the strangest sensation. He felt like he knew it was happening, but he couldn't do anything about it. His thoughts slowed. He wanted to tell someone and say, "Hey mate, I'm going down, you know? I'm fading. Get help."

He might have been mumbling to himself. He couldn't maintain a thought, or keep concentration. He thought he heard an engine or saw a light, but it might just be his mind tricking him. No-one was coming. He was sure. Exposure. What a way to go. Forget the bullets and bombs and beatings. His core temperature was going to sink below the level where it was recoverable and he was simply going to stop functioning. He closed his eyes and felt the cold water on his face. Must lie on my back, he thought. At least I could keep breathing. Like lying on a pillow. He remembered the floatation lessons he had as a child, before he could walk properly. He'd scream bloody murder every time but, now, they might just save his life. He rolled onto his back and felt the cold water slosh around in his ears. It covered his eyes and went up his nose and he snorted it out like a porpoise.

Must not sleep. Must not sl—. Must not ...

CHAPTER THIRTY-FOUR

Hunt saw himself, like he was watching himself from above, an out of body experience. He walked out of a stone cottage, high up on a coastal cliff. He stepped into the mud outside the front door and walked out into the cold and driving rain. He knew where he was going. He knew his mission.

He walked to the top of the cliff face. Big raindrops, like clods of mud, hit his face and body. He yelled out, but the wind buffeting the coast carried his voice away and he was shouting into a void. He looked down at the storm driven waves thumping the cliff. Huge walls of white spray crashed against the rocks down below.

He was going to jump. He knew it. He wasn't afraid. He felt at peace. He would hit the ocean below and be submerged. The strength of the rolling water would hold him down. He would hold his breath and look up at the wash of the breakers above. He would sink down and watch the waves roll in.

Then he heard voices. Somewhere far above him. How could he hear voices if he is under the water. It wasn't English. They were speaking something foreign. An old language rooted in the Caucasus.

"Look! He moved. He's alive."

"Barely."

"Why did you fish him out of the sea?"

"You can't just leave a man to die."

"Did you see the fireball from the helicopter? It was like a film. I've never seen anything like it."

"You're drunk!"

"So what? It's better than the fireworks."

"He needs a doctor."

"No, he needs vodka and a towel."

Just then Hunt's eyes fluttered and his mouth twitched. He tried to speak. His lips chattered and he couldn't get the words out. He realised he was lying on a hard deck. The sickening sway of a boat on a flat sea.

"What's he saying?"

The rest of the group were quiet now. Waiting. Listening. One of them got on their knees and leaned in to hear.

Hunt's voice rasped and hissed, "*Vody*."

"I can't understand you, what?"

"*Vody*," he managed to exhale. Water.

"Water," the guy next to his mouth repeated. "Water. Yes, we are on the water. You are covered in water. It is freezing cold. You nearly died."

"No, you idiot!" another one shouted. "He wants water. He's thirsty."

"Well, why didn't he say so?"

Hunt opened his eyes and the people around him took a quick, scared step back and gasped. He blinked hard. He didn't have the strength to wipe the cold, salty-sea water out of his eyes. His vision was blurry. They were boys rather than men. Young men.

"Come on," one of them said. "Let's take him down below. We need to get him wrapped in a blanket and something warm to drink."

"He's right" said another, "Now we've saved him, we have a responsibility. We can't let him die."

They bent down and picked him up.

"Christ, he's heavy."

"Stop complaining, grab his legs! Be careful with his head."

———

THEY TOOK Hunt below deck and undressed him and wrapped him in a blanket. They gave him a steaming hot mug of coffee from the galley. They sat him up on one of the bunks. His lips were blue. His skin a deathly pale. He couldn't lift the steel mug, so one of the boys helped him wrap his fingers around the tin cup and then turned to the others and said, "His hands are freezing."

They all stood around looking at him under the white ceiling light.

"Who are you?" the tall one at the back asked. "Where are you from? Where can we take you?"

"Sochi," one said. "We can take him back to Sochi."

Hunt tried to shake his head, but it barely moved.

"He's trying to say something. What is it, we can't hear you."

"Odessa," Hunt rasped.

"Odessa!"

"Odessa is too far, we can take you to Russia."

Hunt shook his head. "Not Russia. Georgia ..."

"Georgia!" one exclaimed. "We are from Gagra! On our way home from the celebrations."

Hunt tried to smile. The tall one was enthusiastic.

"This is my brother Levan," he said, touching him on the shoulder. "I am Alek, this is Irakli and this one, Davit."

"Stirling," Hunt said.

"What did he say?" Levan whispered. They all smiled and nodded.

"My father knows a doctor in our hometown," Alek said. "He can help you. After, you can go to Odessa."

THE CLUBHOUSE, LONDON

SOAMES STOOD with his hands behind his back and looked out at the night sky over London Bridge. People were wrapped in scarves and hats against the cold. He wondered where the time went. He hadn't celebrated the new year. He'd been too busy dealing with Scotland Yard over the death of one of his employees. So far, foul play was suspected and, due to a partial thumb print on the murder weapon found at the scene, a rogue MI-6 agent named Stirling Hunt was the main suspect. There was a knock on his office door and without turning around, Soames shouted, "Come!"

He glanced over his shoulder as the door opened a crack and Rishi stuck his head round. Soames turned to greet him and forced a smile. Rishi stepped in.

"Have you heard, sir?" Rishi said. What a ridiculous question. How would he know if he'd heard or not until he told him what it was about. Soames went and sat in his chair and motioned for Rishi to continue.

"Sources are saying he's dead, sir."

"Who?" Soames said through gritted teeth, his patience a mere veneer.

"Hunt, sir. A helicopter was shot down over the Black Sea near Sochi. They're saying it was an accident, but a few eyewitness accounts claim to have heard anti-aircraft fire above the fireworks."

"When was this?" Soames asked.

"A few days ago, sir, on New Year's Eve."

"And we're only hearing about this now. Do they have a body?"

Rishi shook his head, "No, sir, no body. Not yet. Conditions for search and rescue have gotten worse over the last few days. They think they've located the crash site, but nothing concrete so far."

Soames sat looking at his desk.

"It's over, sir."

"What?" Soames asked and furrowed his brow. He hadn't been listening. He was lost in his thoughts.

"It must be over, sir? The search. If Hunt is dead, we don't need to find him anymore."

Soames shook his head.

"If Hunt is dead. He's not dead until they find a body. Not to me, anyway."

Rishi cleared his throat. He stood quietly and waited.

"Is there anything else I can help you with?" Soames asked with a sneer. "If not I suggest you get back to tracking Hunt."

"Ahem, they've pulled our operational budget and reassigned the team," Rishi said.

"What!" Soames slammed his hand on the desk. Rishi jumped and blinked several times.

"Yes, sir, I thought you knew. I presumed you ... the Chief's office reassigned us this morning. I thought it was because the operation was over."

"It's not over! Nothing is over. We have to recover the data!"

Rishi was silent for a second and then asked cautiously, "What data, sir?"

Soames was red faced with anger.

"Something above your pay grade, Rishi. Something I've

been working on in the background. A secret mission. Something you and the higher-ups can never understand. I'm talking about a decryption key that is nothing short of a digital weapon. A weapon that, in the wrong hands, could be extremely valuable. In the hands of the Russian state, catastrophic! The power to steal an entire code base and weaponise it for themselves. We'd be helpless. Powerless! Hunt has the key, I'm sure of it. So you keep working on this, I don't care what the Chief says!"

Rishi stood there looking at Soames and blinking long blinks. He was thinking, but he looked like he was going to fall asleep standing up.

"And you think Stirling has this code, sir?"

"I'm sure of it," Soames said and stood up. He pulled his trousers up at the waist and paced. "Why else would he run? Why else would he kill General Patrick and Tom Holland? Why else would he be in Russia in a helicopter crash?"

"I don't know, sir," Rishi said meekly.

"I do!" Soames said and turned to face him and jabbed himself in the chest. "I do know. So get back to your desk and find out what the hell is going on with the search! This thing isn't over until they find a body. I'll deal with the Chief."

"They're saying Anatoly Mints is in critical condition after being shot in his home too ..." Rishi said.

"What?"

"Anatoly Mints, the Russian Oligarch."

"Yes, I know who it is. You said he was shot."

"Yes, sir, you know what extracting anything from the Russians is like, but it seems one of the guests at his notorious New Year's Eve bashes didn't like the canapés and took it out on him with a nine millimetre pistol."

Soames' face dropped. He suddenly felt pale and light-headed. What did it mean, he wondered.

"I was thinking, sir, it sounds very much like Hunt, doesn't it? Something he would do. If he didn't have the code, he might have been tracking the suspected Russian assassin, the one who he suspected of killing General Patrick."

Soames glanced up at him.

"How did you come by this information?"

"Holland, sir, he kept copious notes. Recorded everything. I was having digital forensics look into the video tape, sir, on Holland's recommendation in his notes. He really was a brilliant investigator, sir, top notch agent. He suspected the video of Hunt to be a fake. A good one, but a fake nonetheless. It might prove the Russians killed the general, which in turn would mean Hunt mightn't have had the intelligence you suspect. He could be the one who killed, or tried to kill, Mints," Rishi said.

Soames was silent.

"You see, sir? It fits."

"Yes," Soames said. "I see." He glared at Rishi. "Now get out of my office and find Hunt's body."

EPILOGUE

Hunt knocked on the apartment door. He listened for a sign of life. Maybe she'd left. It would make sense. He'd brought assassins practically to her door. Then he heard the latch and the door opened a crack. The chain was still on it and he saw Robin's face. Then she realised it was him, the door closed and unlatched again, and swung open.

"Stirling!" she said and her face beamed. She threw her arms wide and jumped up to hug him and wrapped her legs around his waist. She was wearing an oversized shirt and socks.

"I thought you were dead."

He walked inside the flat and closed the door. The cat came up and meowed and rubbed its body on his shin and purred.

"I nearly was."

Robin jumped down and stared at his face and then reached up and grabbed his face and kissed him. It was long and sensual and Hunt was happy to be alive. She pulled back and let go. Her cheeks were flushed.

"I'm happy to see you," she said.

"I'm happy to see you too." And he was.

"You've come back."

"I have ..." he smiled. Then felt bad about getting straight to business. "You haven't sent it, have you?"

"I thought you were dead," she said again. "You told me to send it if anything happened to you. Then the helicopter and the search."

"You sent it?" His heart was racing. "It was a setup," he said. "A mole. My handler was involved. He can't get hold of that key."

"It's in a box on the kitchen counter," she said. "Courier is coming by in an hour. I haven't sent it yet."

Hunt put his hand on his heart and exhaled. "Phew! You had me worried."

"Did I?" she said seductively and walked up to him and pressed her body up against his.

"Yeah, you did."

"How did you survive the crash?"

He shook his head. Hunt had been put up in the cottage at the end of Alek's garden. Their grandmother, a proud Georgian woman in a traditional headscarf and apron looked in on him and brought him hot soup everyday for a week.

"An old grandmother rescued me."

"In a rowing boat?" she asked.

"Something like that," he said.

"What're you going to do, now that you're dead?" Robin asked.

"They think I'm dead?"

She nodded. Hunt lifted his chin to the black box on the counter. "First, we're going to throw that into the sea," he said. "Then I'm going to bury the mole in his hole."

"The mole in his hole?" she said with a smile.

"Yeah," Hunt said and grinned. "Squash him." Then his face was serious. "They have no idea what's coming for them ..."

She looked into his eyes and tiptoed to kiss him again.

THE SERIES CONTINUES ...

Pre-order your copy of **Zambezi Dawn**, book #5 in the Stirling Hunt Mission thriller series, and have it delivered straight to your favourite Kindle device automatically, the moment it's released.

Press on the title to get your copy now:

ZAMBEZI DAWN

ABOUT THE AUTHOR

Stewart Clyde is an Amazon Charts Best Selling author and former army officer.

He has a degree in Politics & International Relations and worked as a journalist. After graduation, he moved to London, and joined the army.

He's lived in eight countries and travelled to over forty. After almost a decade in the Armed Forces, he resigned his commission to write thrillers.

He likes adventures, riding motorcycles through the wine routes of the Iberian Peninsula and the Western Cape, and putting his stories down on paper.

Please get in touch by visiting his website, or on social media:

For more please visit:
www.stewartclydeauthor.com

Join the Stewart Clyde Author Page
on your favourite social media by pressing the button:

Printed in Great Britain
by Amazon

17473906R00144